#1 NATIONAL BESTSELLER

Winner of the Rogers Writers' Trust Fiction Prize
A Globe and Mail **Best Book**

"Every detail of Toews's young heroes' behaviour rings startlingly true and the dialogue is pitch perfect. The premise of the book is sad, yet its execution is filled to the brim with hilarity and joy. Toews captures the rawness of teenagers' personalities—their fledgling attempts at brilliance, their hysterical naiveté and their troubled longings. Toews's book is a love song to young people trying to navigate the volcanic world of adult emotions."
                    —2008 Rogers Writers' Trust Fiction Prize jury

"A book of risk and range without losing any of the wit and warmth that made a bestseller of . . . *A Complicated Kindness.* . . . Toews is an extraordinarily gifted writer."
                    —*The Globe and Mail*

"Not only a fun read with evident literary merit, it has the added advantage of offering a condescension-free view of adolescence."   —*Toronto Star*

"Miriam Toews saunters along the line between comedy and grief as if she might lose her balance at any moment. But she never does. The precarious tone of her novels about fractured families is the crafted effect of a nimble writer. . . . Deadpan irony and hip cultural references abound."   —*The Washington Post*

"Compelling, beautiful and frantic."   —*Vancouver Courier*

"It's darkly funny, bursting at the seams with quirky characters and off-kilter pop culture references that rival Douglas Coupland's for their incisive wit."
—*The Vancouver Sun*

"Compared with Toews's Governor General's Award–winning *A Complicated Kindness*, *The Flying Troutmans* is a lighter, faster read that's not tethered to any particular place or ethnic community. The hum of the road is embedded in the now familiar, deliciously ironic voice."
—*The Gazette*

"Certainly, Anne [of Green Gables] is one of the few children who can hold a candle to Logan, 15, and Thebes, 11, in the new novel by Miriam Toews, *The Flying Troutmans*. . . . You are never sure whether to laugh or cry when reading a Toews book. . . . *The Flying Troutmans* is a dark story but it is also a never-ending series of hilarious adventures."
—*Ottawa Citizen*

"Engaging, humorous, grim and redemptive, this is essential reading."   —*Library Journal*

"While the road-trip story is a common vehicle for the coming-of-age tale, Toews manages to add her own twist to it. . . . Indeed, the strength of the novel is the Troutmans themselves—not to mention Toews's distinctive writing style."   —*Monday Magazine*

"An odd and compelling story about family ties and what happens when they unravel . . . Lest you should think the story is totally depressing, let me say that it's not. It's actually very humorous and touching, in its own peculiar way. Toews's fearless writing style and offbeat imagination are wonderful. Don't miss this one."

—*Metro Valley Newspaper Group*

"Not since Stephen Leacock have our neighbours to the north given us a writer as witty and wise as Miriam Toews."

—*Los Angeles Times*

"*The Flying Troutmans* is a fitting continuation of Toews's body of work. Once again she captures the soul of the clever teenager overcoming huge odds. She shines a kindly light on family dynamics that the average social worker would find worthy of a hefty investigation. And she balances heartbreak with laugh-out-loud wit."

—*Edmonton Journal*

"Toews writes . . . in a high-energy original voice filled with love, fear, humour and originality. This energetic originality does have literary sisters and brothers: Sherman Alexie, Billie Livingston, Emma Richler, Zoe Whittall, Thomas King and the inevitable J. D. Salinger come immediately to mind. The power-thrust, the growing pains, the humour, the surprises and the layering are core to all of the above."

—*The Globe and Mail*

T. F. T.

the Flying TROUTMANS

MIRIAM TOEWS

VINTAGE CANADA

VINTAGE CANADA EDITION, 2009

Published in Canada by Vintage Canada, a division of Random House
of Canada Limited, Toronto, in 2009. Originally published in
hardcover in Canada by Alfred A. Knopf Canada, a division
of Random House of Canada Limited, in 2008. Distributed by
Random House of Canada Limited, Toronto.

Vintage Canada and colophon are registered trademarks of
Random House of Canada Limited.

www.randomhouse.ca

The author acknowledges with gratitude the support of the
Manitoba Arts Council and the Canada Council for the Arts.

LIBRARY AND ARCHIVES CANADA CATALOGUING IN PUBLICATION

Toews, Miriam, 1964–
The flying Troutmans / Miriam Toews.

ISBN 978-0-307-40090-1

I. Title.

PS8589.O6352F59 2009   C813'.54   C2008-905501-2

Book design by Kelly Hill

Printed and bound in the United States of America

2 4 6 8 9 7 5 3 1

for kaya, owen
and georgia (100% b.a.)

one

YEAH, SO THINGS HAVE FALLEN APART. A few weeks
ago I got a collect call from my niece, Thebes, in the middle of the night, asking me to please come back to help
with Min. She told me she'd been trying to take care of
things but it wasn't working any more. Min was stranded
in her bed, hooked on blue torpedoes and convinced that
a million silver cars were closing in on her (I didn't know

what Thebes meant either), Logan was in trouble at school, something about the disturbing stories he was writing, Thebes was pretending to be Min on the phone with his principal, the house was crumbling around them, the back screen door had blown off in the wind, a family of aggressive mice was living behind the piano, the neighbours were pissed off because of hatchets being thrown into their yard at all hours (again, confusing, something to do with Logan) . . . basically, things were out of control. And Thebes is only eleven.

I told her I'd be there as soon as I could. I had no choice. There was no question. Our parents are dead. Min didn't have anybody else. And in just about every meaningful way, neither did I. Admittedly, I would have preferred to keep roaming around Paris pretending to be an artist with my moody, adjective-hating boyfriend, Marc, but he was heading off to an ashram in India anyway and said we could communicate telepathically. I tried it a couple of days before he left. I love you, don't go, I said silently, without moving my lips. He was standing next to me, trying to photograph a gargoyle. You're a little in my way, he said. Can you move? No amount of telepathy worked with him, but maybe you have to be thousands of miles away from someone in order for your thoughts to work up the speed and velocity required to hit their target.

At the airport, Thebes came running over to me dressed entirely in royal blue terry cloth, short shorts and cropped top, and covered in some kind of candy necklace powder.

The empty elastic was still around her throat. Or maybe she wore that thing all the time. She had fake tattoos all over her arms and her hair was intense purple, matted and wild, and she melted into me when I put my arms around her and tried to lift her off the ground.

Hey, you crazy kid, I said. How are you? She couldn't talk because she was crying too hard. How are you, Thebie? I asked again. How are things? I didn't have to ask her. I had a pretty good idea. I let her wrap herself around me and then I carried her over to a plastic airport chair, sat down with her sprawled in my lap, all arms and legs, like a baby giraffe, and let her cry.

How's the songwriting going? I finally whispered in her ear. I really liked that line . . . take a verse, Mojo . . . you know? I said. She was always e-mailing me her lyrics and cc'ing David Geffen on them.

She frowned. She wiped the snot off her face with the back of her hand, then onto her shorts. I'm more into martial arts now, and yo-yoing, she said. I need to get out of my head.

Yeah, I said. Using your kung fu powers for good?

Well, she said, I feel good when I flip people.

Hey, I said, where's your brother?

She told me he was outside waiting in the van because he didn't know how to work the parking and also he didn't actually have his driver's licence, only his learner's, he's fifteen, he's all jacked up on rebellion and whatever, he just wanted to wait in the van and listen to his music.

We headed for the exit and kind of stumbled around, falling over each other. Thebes kept her arm wrapped around my waist and tried to help me with my bag. All I had was one large backpack. I didn't know how long I'd be staying but it didn't really matter anyway. I'd lost my boyfriend and didn't care about my job and there was no reason to go back to Paris. I didn't own anything besides books, and Marc could keep those if he wanted to.

It was sunny and warm and the sky was a sharp, cartoony blue compared to the wet clay skies of Paris, and there was Logan sitting in their beat-up van staring straight ahead at something, not us, music blasting from inside, like the van was a giant Marshall amp. Thebes ran up to the van and threw herself against the windshield. Logan snapped out of his rock 'n' roll reverie for a second and smiled. Then he got out of the van and walked, glided, over to me and gave me a big hug with one arm and asked me how it was going.

All right, I said, how about you?

Mmmm, he said. He shrugged.

Hey, what's this? I asked him. I grabbed his arm and squeezed his bicep.

Yeah, right, said Thebes.

And, dude, your pants! I said. Did you steal them from Andre the Giant? I snapped the elastic band on his boxers. Logan opened the door to the van and threw my stuff in.

How was Paris? he asked.

What? I said. Oh, Paris?

Yeah, he said. How was it?

Thebes turned down the volume on the music. Then she told me I should drive instead of Logan. She said she'd been planning her funeral on the way there.

I got dumped, I said.

No way! said Logan.

Well, yeah, I said.

You can't get *dumped* in Paris, said Logan. Isn't it supposed to be all—

By a guy or a girl? asked Thebes.

A guy, I said.

Logan stared hard at Thebes for a few seconds. He said you were gay, she said.

No I didn't, said Logan.

You totally did! said Thebes.

Okay, Thebes, listen, said Logan. I didn't—

Hey, I said. It's okay. It really doesn't matter. Really. But it was a guy.

But you're not that old, said Thebes, right? You can still find someone if you look hard. How old are you?

Twenty-eight, I said.

Okay, twenty-eight, she said. She thought for a second. You have like two years, she said. Maybe you should dress up more, though.

Logan ended up driving back to their house because I didn't know how to tell him not to and because he hadn't seemed interested in relinquishing control of the wheel anyway. Logan and Thebes yelled at each other all the way back, the music cranked the whole time.

Thebes: Stay in your lane, moron!

Logan: Don't lose your fucking shit, man!

Thebes: I don't want to die, loser! Use two hands!

Logan: Do NOT grab the steering wheel!

Then Thebes went into this strange kind of commentary thing she does, quoting the imaginary people in her head. This time it was a funeral director, I think. She said: With an impact this severe there is not a hope of reconstructing this kid's face. She banged the back window with her fist.

What was that? I asked her.

The lid of my coffin slamming down, she said. Closed casket. I'll be unrecognizable anyway.

It was great to see the kids again. They'd changed a bit, especially Logan. He was a young man now, not a child. More on his mind, maybe, but with less compulsion to share it. Thebes was more manic than the last time I'd seen her. I knew what that was about. It's hard not to get a little hysterical when you're trying desperately to keep somebody you love alive, especially when the person you're trying to save is ambivalent about *being* saved. Thebes reminded me of myself when I was her age, rushing home from school ahead of Min so I could create the right vibe, a mood of happiness and fun that would sustain her for another day, or so I thought. I'd mentally rehearse what I thought were amusing anecdotes to entertain her, make her laugh. I didn't know then that all my ridiculous efforts only brought her further down. Sometimes she would laugh or applaud half-heartedly, but it was always with an expression that said, yeah, whatever, Hattie, nice try, but everything is bullshit.

—

My birth triggered a seismic shift in my sister's life. The day I was born she put her dress on backwards and ran away towards a brighter future, or possibly towards a brighter past. Our parents found her in a tree next door. Had she been planning to jump? She's been doing that ever since, travelling in two opposite directions at once, towards infancy and death. I don't know exactly what it was about me. By all accounts before I existed Min was a normal little girl, normal enough. She could pick a direction and stick with it. Our family photo albums are filled, halfway, with shots of Min laughing and smiling and enjoying life. And then, suddenly, I'm in the picture and Min's joy evaporates. I've spent hours staring at those photos trying to understand my sister. Even in the ones in which I don't appear it's easy to see by Min's expression that I am just beyond the lens, somewhere nearby.

Min's had good days, some inexplicable breaks from the madness, periods of time where she functions beautifully and life is as smooth as glass, almost. The thing I remember most clearly about Cherkis, Thebes's and Logan's dad, is how nuts he was about Min and how excited he'd get when Min was on the up-and-up, taking care of business and acting normal. I liked that about him, but it also broke my heart because he had no idea of the amount of shit that was about to fly. Eventually, though, he did come to understand, and he did what I did, and what so many others in her life have done.

He left.

Min had a vague notion of where he'd gone. At first it was Tokyo, about as far away as you can get from here without being on your way back. He moved around the Pacific Rim, and then Europe for a while, South America, and then South Dakota. He'd call sometimes to see how the kids were doing, how Min was doing, if she wanted him to come back. No, she didn't, she said, every time. And if he tried to take the kids she'd kill herself for real. We didn't know whether this was a bluff or not, but nobody wanted to challenge it. They were all she had, she told him. Cherkis wasn't the type of guy to hire a lawyer and fight for custody. He told Min he'd wait until the kids were old enough to decide for themselves and take things from there. He didn't want to rock Min's boat. He didn't want anybody getting hurt.

I moved to Paris, fled Min's dark planet for the City of Lights. I didn't want to leave her and the kids but the truth is she scared me and I thought she might be better off without me, too. Especially if I was the embodiment of her particular anguish. It had been hard to know whether to stay or go.

It's impossible to move through the stages of grief when a person is both dead and alive, the way Min is. It's like she's living permanently in an airport terminal, moving from one departure lounge to another but never getting on a plane. Sometimes I tell myself that I'd do anything for Min. That I'd do whatever was necessary for her to be happy. Except that I'm not entirely sure what that would be.

So the next best thing to being dead was being far away, at least as far as Paris. I had a boyfriend, Marc, and a job in a bookstore, and occasionally I'd go home, back to Manitoba, to Min and Thebes and Logan, for Christmas or the odd birthday, or to help with Min if she was in a really bad patch, but of course that was complicated because I never knew whether I should be there or not.

I wanted to be an artist, in Paris, or a psychiatrist. Sometimes I'd haul a giant pad of sketch paper and some charcoal pencils to the square in front of the Louvre or wherever the tourists were and I'd offer to sketch them for free. I didn't feel right about charging anybody, because I wasn't really doing a good job. In every sketch, it didn't matter if I was drawing the face of a man or a woman or a kid, I'd include a detail from Min's face, from what I could remember at that precise moment. Sometimes it was the shape of her eyebrows, or her wide lips, or a constellation of tiny freckles, or even just a shadow beneath the cheekbone. The people I sketched were always slightly confused and disappointed when I showed them my work, I could tell, but most of them were kind, especially because I didn't expect any payment.

Our father died in a drowning accident in Acapulco when Min and I were kids. He drowned trying to save us. We'd been racing and had swum out farther than we should have and Min had started panicking, screaming for help. The current was strong and we couldn't get back to the shore no matter how hard we pushed against the water.

I remember yelling at Min to move sideways and to let go of me. After that, my memory of events is blurry. I have a feeling that Min was pushing me down, under water. I think that I remember her hand on my head, or on my shoulder, but maybe I'm wrong. Our mother told us that Dad had heard our screams and had swum out to get us, but that he too had got caught in the undertow and disappeared. They said it was a riptide. Other people on the beach eventually grabbed a boat from somewhere and rescued us, but by then Dad was gone. Min was fifteen and I was nine. They left us lying in the sun on the beach, crying and vomiting up salt water, while they searched for him.

You ready? asked Thebes.

Yup, I said, and we went into the house and up to Min's bedroom. Logan stayed downstairs in the living room and put on some music.

Min was lying in her bed under a white sheet. She looked like a kid, she'd lost so much weight. I could see the bumps of her kneecaps and hip bones poking up beneath the sheet. Nothing else. Her eyes were big and wild and blue. Her face was pale and waxy and her hands lay palms-up at her sides. There was a powerfully stale smell in the room. She smiled, barely.

Min, I said. Min. I'm here now. I smiled back and kissed her very gently and held her hand, and then her head, and then I kissed her again.

Please don't touch me, she whispered. It hurts too much.

Can I try? I said. If I try to be more gentle? I sat down on the bed and Min grimaced. I apologized and stood up. She smiled and glanced briefly at her hand. Thebes told me I could hold my hand over hers without touching it. A gesture. Your fingernails are so long, I said. I smiled. You could be a hand model. Do you want me to trim them? She blinked, no.

Everything hurts her, said Thebes. Eating hurts her. Walking hurts her. Even drops of water.

I go to Aviva and buy her six vanilla shakes. I can fit them all into my carrier. She only eats soft food. Thebes said she had to hold the shake for Min and Min would sip slowly from the straw and Thebes would sing.

Would you like the window open a tiny bit? I asked Min. She stared at me and then looked at Thebes.

No, she doesn't, said Thebes. She's worried about getting a chill.

The music stopped downstairs and the TV came on, briefly. I heard Dr. Phil screaming at a woman for not loving herself more. Then the TV was off too, and the music was back on.

Logan has total electronic domination in this house, said Thebes, like it was an *Animal Kingdom* fact. She scurried around the room humming and lining up pill bottles and gathering up used tissues and milkshake containers and making sure she didn't accidentally bump Min's bed. I stood next to Min and she and I stared at each other.

I painted her room for her, said Thebes. I was trying to jazz it up and make it cheerful. She'd used some kind of sponge technique and there were blotches of red all over the yellow walls. Logan says it looks like somebody blew their brains out in here but I think it's pretty, she said. And, Mom, you do too, right? Min smiled again and closed her eyes. She does, said Thebes.

I talked for a while. I told Min about Paris, about my boyfriend, my job, about a bunch of stuff, and then I asked her if there was a bed ready for her at the hospital. She looked at Thebes again.

Yeah, said Thebes, I think so.

So, we should go, I said. Thebes had packed up some things for Min in her old Little Mermaid backpack. She likes oceans, said Thebes. She wants to bob along the surface of things.

That's sweet, Thebes, I said. I didn't mention that mermaids generally hang out at the bottom of the sea. She knew it herself, anyway. I imagined my father's body being buffeted along the sandy bottom of the Pacific Ocean, bumping up against reefs and fish and shipwrecks, always on the move. As if he was still alive but in another world, like Min. She was a strange, unsettled planet that had once sustained life. She was a language that I had thought I almost understood even though I couldn't speak it. She hadn't always been this way. She used to wear high knee socks and short shorts and tube tops, and travel everywhere on roller skates. If our parents took us horseback riding, she'd pick the wildest horse and have it tamed in five seconds, flying joyously across fields and through rivers and leaping over fences. She taught me how to bumper-shine and cannonball and roll a joint and make a homemade bong. She went barefoot from May to October and once, on a dare, swam across Falcon Lake in the middle of the night.

At that resort in Acapulco, before our father drowned, Min owned the place. She wore a string bikini made out of purple glass beads, army boots and a black Labatt toque over her long, blonde hair. She lounged around all day on the beach reading *Quotations from Chairman Mao, The Anarchist Cookbook* and *Paradise Lost*. She smoked beedies that she shoplifted from a store called Orientique. Sometimes she'd bury me in the sand. Sometimes we'd race in the water. Can you hold this for me? she'd say to anyone who was around. She'd stick her book and her beedies into her toque and hand it to them and then sashay like a supermodel across the sand and into the water to cool off. I would stand on the beach squinting into the sun and watch her and count the number of seconds she stayed under water. One thousand. Two thousand. Three thousand . . . I knew that any number over thirty spelled disaster, and I'd sidle closer and closer to the water so I could be the one to rescue her.

I'd show you our plecostamus, said Thebes, but we haven't seen him in four months. She was talking about their fish, a bottom-feeder. Logan feeds him every night, she said, but he has to turn the light off first so nobody sees him when he grabs his pellet of food. That's the only way he'll eat it. Thebes told me she sometimes tried to stay up all night to catch him swimming but it never worked.

Our only pet ever, she said, and we never see him. I wondered if their poor plecostamus was dead. How much faith does it require to feed a fish you haven't seen in four months? Other people's plecostamuses grow to be *this big,* said Thebes, holding her hands about eight inches apart. But our little guy doesn't do a thing. She and I stared at the murky water in the aquarium.

Should it be cleaned? I asked her.

I'm afraid to, she said.

Min was weak and starving and could barely walk. Logan carried her to the van, no sweat, lighter than his backpack, almost, he said, and sat squished in a corner of the back seat with Min stretched out and her head in his lap on the way to the hospital.

Don't worry about a thing, he told her. She looked up at him. You'll be back, he said. You'll get better. He stared out the window and smiled and drummed his fingers against the glass and cleared his throat several times. He stroked Min's hair, awkwardly, beautifully, and then stopped but didn't seem to know where to put his hand. I drove and Thebes rode shotgun, and she told me that I was an excellent driver, very prudent, very defensive, *everyone* should drive as well as I do, and then looked over her shoulder at Logan, who didn't notice because he was busy trying to hide his tears.

At the hospital a big guy whose name tag said "Bernie" checked Min in and told her she'd be safe there.

She was safe at home, said Thebes.

Bernie ignored her. What's your mood like, Min? he said.

She looked at Thebes.

Her mood? said Thebes.

How's she feeling right now? he said. Min stared at him. Okay, good stuff, said Bernie. A parade of patients shuffled past us for their hourly smoke and Min slowly got up out of her chair and started to walk towards the elevators.

Oops, nope, said Bernie. This way, sweetie. Then he asked us if Min had any sharps or fire or belts or shoelaces on her, and Thebes told Bernie to ask Min herself. Good stuff, said Bernie again.

Min tried wandering over to the elevators again, but this time I took her hand and kept her close to me.

Logan had disappeared inside his hoodie and giant pants. His headphones were around his neck but I could hear the music faintly. He cracked his knuckles a few times and stared out the window. Then he smiled at Min and shrugged and smiled again. We heard someone moaning and a nurse saying, That's enough, in a loud, too loud, voice. Like she was so sure of the limits, but the limits to what?

Fucking nightmare on Elm Street, eh, Mom? said Logan. Min closed her eyes and opened them.

Why aren't you at the beach, said Logan and Thebes in unison, which I found out later was some kind of in-joke because the last time they had to bring Min to the hospital it was a really hot day and everyone in the waiting room was hiding behind newspapers that said in giant black letters, Why Aren't You at the Beach?

Min was checked in. We walked with her to her room and stood around her bed for a few minutes. Hey, I said, this will be great, Min, this is . . . look, here's a button you push for help. She closed her eyes. Thebes unpacked her Little Mermaid backpack and put a photograph of her and Logan and Min, smiling, laughing, even Logan, on the bedside table. She pulled out one of Min's pillboxes and opened it up and showed it to me. She'd replaced the pills with tiny cinnamon hearts, one for every day of the week.

They'll give her new ones here, she said. Right, Min? Min didn't say anything. Right, Thebes, said Thebes. She wrote a note on a piece of paper and stuck it into the cardboard frame. *We love you, Mom, and we always will. You're the best mom in the world. We love you!!!* Min opened her eyes again, smiled and patted the bed for Thebes to sit down beside her, but gently, very gently.

Min looked at me and crooked her finger. She wanted to talk to me. I put my head next to hers and she whispered in my ear.

Logan leaned against the wall and fiddled around with his headphones.

A bald head popped around the curtain and said, Hello, my name is Jeanette. We all said hello and she told us she was Min's roommate. She was a really heavy breather. She was wearing dark shades and a Superman T-shirt and no pants. Min raised her hand and then let it fall back onto the bed. Jeanette told us she'd been there for thirteen weeks. She'd had lots of different roommates. She said she stayed in shape by walking the halls, incessantly. She'd been a military supplier. She'd look out for Min. She said it was nice that Min had this little family to visit her. Jeanette's family weren't allowed to visit her, she said, because they made her too agitated.

Okay, thank you, it's nice meeting you, too. I turned back to my sister. Min, I said. Hey, Min. There was something I wanted to tell her, too. But she was out, fast asleep, or zonked on whatever Bernie had given her when she arrived. I leaned over and whispered into her ear. No, never, I said.

Logan and Thebes stood there staring at her and then Logan pulled the blanket up so it covered her shoulders and Thebes moved the family photo a fraction of an inch on the bedside table, lining it up with Min's eyes so it would be the first thing she'd see when the drugs wore off.

A woman asked to speak to me in the hall. She was a social worker. She asked me if I knew of any arrangements that had been made for the children, and I told her yes, I had come from Europe to look after them for as long as they needed me to. The words sounded as though they belonged to somebody else, or like I was reading from a teleprompter or a karaoke screen.

The social worker said that was good but they might have to conduct a home assessment and perhaps a background check on me to make sure I was competent and didn't have any outstanding arrest warrants or my name on any abuse registries. That's fine, I said, but Logan and Thebes can't go to a foster home.

Well, said the woman, very likely not, but that would have to be determined by others. I thanked her for her concern. She thanked me for my understanding of the situation. We shook hands.

two

WHEN WE GOT BACK TO THE HOUSE Logan grabbed
his basketball, threw it really hard against the hallway wall,
knocked the framed family photo to the floor—it didn't
break, he didn't pick it up—and then left with a couple of
his friends. Thebes picked up the photo, hung it back on
the wall, sighed heavily like she'd travelled to every corner
of the world, on her knees, with a knife in her back and a

boa constrictor wrapped around her chest, and then made us a couple of blueberry smoothies.

The phone rang.

Don't answer it, said Thebes. We're screening. It was the principal of Logan's school again, wanting to know what was up, when he could get together with Logan's mom for a chat. Thebes and I stood next to the phone and listened to him talk. He asked if they had moved, if this was still their number. He didn't want to be pushy, he said, but it was really important that he and Logan's mother have a conversation.

Should I pick it up? I asked Thebes.

No! she said. She told me I had to go and be Min.

Yeah, but doesn't he know what she looks like? I asked her.

No, he's clueless, she said.

Yeah, but can't I just go and be myself and explain the situation, that Min's in the hospital?

No, said Thebes. No, she said again. She shook her head slowly, gravely. She didn't want to go to a foster home.

You won't go to a foster home! I said. I'm here to take care of you.

Yeah, she said, but for how long?

I tried to reassure her. I tried to convince her that she wasn't going to a foster home, but I knew my tone was tentative and that she was having a hard time believing me.

Cross your heart and hope to die? she said. I wondered how often, on average, a parent makes a preposterous promise to a kid and then begins to panic.

Well, yeah, I said. Definitely.

———

Thebes and I sat at the kitchen table and drank our blueberry shakes. She told me about some of the stories Logan had been writing in English class. The principal is worried about him, she said. She told me that Logan had almost gotten suspended for telling the principal he was lame, or his jokes were, or something like that. And that the principal had told him to smarten up and then Logan had said he hated that expression, *smarten up,* because it makes the person saying it sound like an imbecile.

It's kind of true, though, I said.

Do you miss your boyfriend? asked Thebes.

Yeah, kind of, I said.

Are you sad? she asked.

I am, yeah, I said. But I'm okay. I told her she looked a little tired.

No, she wasn't tired, but we could lie down on the living room floor if *I* was tired.

Thebes and I lay on the living room floor and talked. Well, she talked. She talked about her friends. We're all mostly white nerds, she said, with minor physical and emotional flaws that do not require medication but do brand us as losers in the bigger picture.

Who's Mojo? I asked her. She had mentioned him, or her, in some of her e-mails.

My imaginary bandmate, she said. Bass player.

She talked about the purple bulges under Min's eyes, how they were getting bigger and bigger. How Min had tried, in the beginning, to cover them up with some makeup but it was too light and she looked like she had a goggles tan. Sometimes at night, said Thebes, before she stopped getting out of bed completely, I could hear her pacing downstairs, humming to herself, making cup after cup of camomile tea. Or playing darts by herself in the basement. Thebes described the way it sounded. Three small *thunks,* she said, the darts hitting the target, and then approximately eleven or twelve seconds of silence while Min walked to the dartboard, removed the darts and returned to the throwing line. Then three more *thunks,* and another eleven or twelve seconds of silence. Over and over, like someone knocking softly, patiently, but persistently on the front door.

She told me about a city in India where monkeys are a holy manifestation of some god and are allowed to run wild wherever they want to go. One of them stole a tourist's glasses and there was nothing the cops could do, she said. What I would have done, she said, is look for the monkey wearing glasses and then try to exchange them for something else. What was your boyfriend's name? she asked me.

Marc, I said.

Did you want to get married?

No.

Why not?

I'm . . . I don't know.

Did he?

No.

Was he good-looking?

No, not particularly. Not conventionally.

Was he good at sports?

I don't know.

Did you know I had an operation on my brain and part of the scalpel broke off and is still in there?

Yeah, I had known, Min had told me.

Logan tried to stick magnets to my head, said Thebes. Thebes had become a talking machine. Maybe she was attempting to use up all the words that Min had left behind, taking whatever popped into her head, any thought, idea or fact, and transforming it into sound, noise, life. She was talking for two, in double time.

When we were kids, Min would go for months without saying a word. Her muteness was her voice, her retreat was her attack. It was all upside down and disconcerting and it had made me nuts. I used to do the same thing that Thebes was doing now, blather away non-stop about anything that came to mind, and really it was only when I got to Paris and Marc told me that silence was golden, especially mine, that I realized how much I talked.

Do you want to watch TV? I asked her. There was a thick layer of dust on the screen. Someone had written *Deborah Solomon, be my girlfriend* in the dust. Or, hey, maybe you should have a nice, hot bath.

She said she was too nervous to stop talking. She wanted to talk. She *had* to talk. She got up and walked around while she talked. Hopped onto the couch and off again. She told me about Logan's X-rated stories, the ones he had been getting in trouble for. The last one had been about a boy who was disturbed from having to listen to his mom having "mind-blowing sex" with her new boyfriend, and from then walking in on his dad, who'd just hung himself. She said Min had been upset by it. She imitated Min being upset. Logan, she said, we talked about this stuff. Can't you just . . . You're making me . . . These stories are not . . . , said Thebes. It was an uncannily accurate impersonation. It was obvious that Thebes had been spending a lot of time observing her mother, trying to understand, trying to find a way in. It was the same thing I'd been doing all my life.

Thebes yanked at her purple hair and groaned. We were quiet, thinking of Min.

You know, she used to write kind of racy stories herself, I told Thebes. But she could get away with anything at school because all the teachers were afraid of her.

Why were they afraid of her? said Thebes.

Well, not afraid of her, I said. They were *wary* of her. She had this ability to make every outrageous thing she did seem prescient, as though it would be the thing that all enlightened people would soon be doing and wondering why they hadn't thought of it first. Which was great, I said, but also lonely. For her. It reads well in a biography but it doesn't make real life easy. You know how most parents encourage their kids to be themselves, to speak their minds and not follow the crowd? Well, our parents did the opposite with Min. They begged her to succumb to peer pressure. To follow the pack and be content with it. Let other people get ideas first, they'd say. Wait around for normal people to map things out. They'd say it jokingly, with their arms around her.

Thebes stood still for at least seven seconds. I had said the wrong thing again. I had implied that radical thinkers automatically go crazy, which wasn't true, and definitely wouldn't be any consolation to a kid like Thebes. I wanted to say something else, to take it back and start again, but then she told me about another story Logan had written.

It revolved around a man who worked in a paper factory and became so bored he decided to set a goal. He'd become the fattest man in the world. It went on about the inner workings of this guy's brain, how some parts were overdeveloped and some not at all and the guy wondered why, if it was something that occurred in his childhood, or because there were only women in his life.

Hmm, I said. I didn't know either. At least he had a goal.

I was so tired. I'd been dumped for Buddha. I had jet lag. I'd just put my sister into a psych ward. I was suddenly responsible for two kids, one who hardly talked and one who couldn't stop, with no clue how to take care of either of them.

Hey, said Thebes, what did Min whisper in your ear at the hospital?

Nothing, I said.

Yeah, she did, said Thebes. I saw her whisper something in your ear. What?

I can't remember, I said.

Yeah, you can, said Thebes. C'mon. Think. She stood over me, a scrawny leg on either side. She still had streaks of candy necklace powder all over her face and neck. She pointed her finger at me like a gun. Tell me! she said in one of her character voices, or I'll go right ahead and bust a cap in your ass.

She said we should find your father, I said.

That wasn't true. I had made it up on the spot. Please help me die, is what she'd actually whispered in my ear. And I had said, No, never. Was that the right thing to say? I don't know. I remember standing outside Min's bedroom door, I was probably around twelve years old, and hearing my mother telling her that if she really, seriously, genuinely wanted to die, there was absolutely nothing that my mother could do to stop her and she would be devastated but she would give Min her blessing and she would love her forever. It bothered me. No, I thought, that's not the thing to tell Min. Tell her she can't die. Absolutely not. No fucking way. We had every way of stopping her and we'd never let her go. But now I'm not so sure. There is not one single thing that I am certain of, except that I have to make sure Thebes and Logan are taken care of. But not necessarily by me.

Did she really say that? asked Thebes. She sat down beside me on the floor.

Yeah, she did, I told her.

Really?

Really. Yeah.

Why?

Because, Thebes, she understands now just how sick she is and that she needs Cherkis to help her out.

With me and Logan? said Thebes.

Yeah, I said.

But I don't want to live with Cherkis, said Thebes. I want to live with Min.

I know that, I said. Don't worry. If we found Cherkis we would just ask him if he wanted to come back here to take care of you for a while.

But Min doesn't want to see him, said Thebes.

I know, I said, that's true, but I think she's realizing that she needs some help.

Yeah, said Thebes, but you're here.

Yeah, I said. I know . . . that's true too.

I wished my mother was alive. She could tell me what to do. Or she could do it herself. She knew how to talk to Min and bring her down to earth, at least most of the time. She absorbed Min's despair but recycled it into dark comedy, or something. She'd joke around with Min about death and hopelessness, and Min would respond. In a way it was like Min's own theory that everything is bullshit, except that my mother took it one healthy step further: yup, everything is bullshit but it's also funny. She died two years ago from a ruptured aorta, her heart exploded, but neither Min nor I found it all that hysterical.

Anyway, I didn't want to be here. I didn't know how to talk to the kids. I loved them, but I didn't want to live with my sister. Even in her weakest, most defeated and delusional moments Min was in control. If she was again at that point where she wanted to die, where she was begging me to help her die, then there was no point in keeping Cherkis at bay. What difference did it make? I had no idea whether Cherkis would be interested in seeing his kids again, let alone moving back and taking care of them, but he was a decent human being, a caring guy. He was their father. He had loved them once and could again, or maybe he still did but from a distance. A safe distance. If there is such a thing.

So, said Thebes, is that what we're going to do? Find Cherkis?

I think we'll try, I said. How does that sound to you?

Thebes said she didn't know. Good, she guessed, probably, it was strange, kind of exciting, a little weird, she'd probably get a stomach ache, no, it was good, just a small stomach ache, yeah, it would be fine. Probably. If that was what Min really wanted.

Well, yeah, I said. It is. *And I'm so sorry for lying to you.*

Later that evening I lay down in Min's empty bed upstairs and pulled her white sheet up over my head. I felt for my kneecaps and hip bones. I lay perfectly still, arms down, palms up. I closed my eyes and pretended I was floating in space, then at sea, then not floating at all. I hummed an old Beach Boys tune. *In my room* . . . Min had taught me how to play it on her guitar when we were kids. I opened my eyes and stared at her pill bottles and squinted until they all blurred together. I stopped squinting and lined up the bottles, smallest to biggest, in rows, like a class photo. All her life Min had been surrounded by pills and sometimes she took them and sometimes she didn't and sometimes she took way too many of them. She'd always keep one small, blue pill under her pillow, like a tooth. Or a cyanide capsule right there at the ready.

I remembered the time she had agreed to go rabbit hunting with our uncle and was so horrified by the idea of killing something that she consumed an entire jar of my aunt's diet pills so that her aim would be way off and the rabbits would escape. But Min, my mother had said, you could have said no, or intentionally misfired. You almost killed yourself in order not to kill a rabbit? That just doesn't make any sense.

I turned on Min's radio, heard someone laughing and turned it off again. There was still paint on it from when she and I, as teenagers, spent a summer painting a giant dairy barn. We painted in our bathing suits, and made scaffolding for ourselves from giant tractor tires and two-by-fours. We played the radio all day and knew the words to every song. Min fell hard for one of the farmhands and ended up getting pregnant after seeing *Raiders of the Lost Ark*. She lost the farmhand's tiny embryo a month or so later in the washroom of a bar called Club Soda, and cried for days and days, and then stopped talking. Sometimes, before I went to bed, I would tap the wall between our bedrooms, and sometimes she'd tap back, very softly, but mostly she didn't, and eventually I stopped tapping too.

I lay in Min's bed and tried really hard not to think about Marc, about his soft kisses and how his arm felt around my shoulders and the way he breathed when we made love and the way he hopped around when he was happy and the stuff he said about my eyes and my hips and the small of my back, and what the hell can an ashram offer that I can't? I mean besides silence and solitude and spiritual revitalization. I tried to float again. I could hear Thebes and her friend rehearsing *When I Go Mad,* a horror play about an insane mother that they were planning to put on for the neighbour kids. They used British accents. Thebes was the insane mother. Here's a snippet.

Thebes: Good night, dahling, I'm off to the bar.
Friend: New, new, Mutha, please sing to me first.
Thebes: Oooookay, I shall siiiiing to you, yeeees, of course, but while I sing you must close your eyes.

Then there's the murder attempt and the screaming part, which they were having a really hard time getting through without laughing. They were already on take thirty-five or something.

I got up and knocked on Thebes's door. There were Groovy Girls stickers all over the door and goofy photos of her and her friends.

Bonjourno! Thebes said. C'mon in. Take five, Abbey, she said to her friend. Thebes was wearing this glittery silver sash that she had ripped off a fake Christmas present when they were in Mexico one year, and her friend was wearing one of Thebes's old Winnie-the-Pooh nightgowns over her jeans. They were flushed and out of breath from all that psychotic killing and bar-hopping.

When does Logan usually get home? I asked her.

Eleven is his curfew during the week, but he ignores it, she said. She was reapplying her lipstick, using a CD as a mirror. Abbey was curled up in the fetal position on the bed. Archie comics were everywhere, walls of them, and a big hardcover called *A Criminal History of Mankind* propped the window open.

When he gets home, we're gonna talk about this whole deal, I said.

Thebes was warming to the idea of looking for Cherkis. She thought he was a poet but she didn't know exactly. She remembered seeing him when she was three or four, after her operation when the piece of scalpel broke off in her brain.

I went into Logan's room for a look around. There were books and CDs all over the floor and band posters covering the walls. I stared back at the naked guy in the Pixies poster giving the thumbs-down to the world. On the wall by his bed Logan had written a poem or a mission statement or a prayer or something in very tiny letters that slanted down, down, and farther down, until one line obliterated the next.

Be nicer to people

Be nicer to people

Be nicer to people

Be nicer to people

Be nicer to people

Be nicer to people

Be nicer to people

You're not stylish or cool

Be nicer to people

Be nicer to people

Be nicer to people

three

THAT NIGHT LOGAN CAME HOME DRUNK. I heard him fall down in the kitchen. I went in and switched on the light and he said, Oh man, dude, that is a seriously diaphanous nightgown you've got on. I switched the light off again and knelt down beside his head. C'mon, let's get you up to bed. He wanted to stay there.

What's that smell? he asked.

Cascade, I said. C'mon, let's go. He pawed at the box of Cascade and spilled it all over the floor and himself.

Shit, he said. Thebes came downstairs rubbing her eyes, *still* covered in candy necklace crap, and asked us what was up.

We're at the beach, said Logan. Check out the sand. He moved his fingers around in the Cascade crystals.

Logan's hammered, I said. Help me get him up to bed. She grabbed one of his feet and began to drag him across the kitchen floor and down the hall.

Okay, okay, don't, don't, he said. I'll walk. He rambled on about renaming the thumb. We should totally rename the thumb, just the three of us, tonight!

What do you want to call it? asked Thebes.

Renée! said Logan. No, Shenée! Yeah . . .

We helped him up the stairs and pushed him onto his bed. He fell face down, and I punched the pillow next to his head so he'd have an air hole. Thebes took off his shoes and a condom fell out of one of them.

Yeah, right, she said.

Does he have a girlfriend? I asked her.

Deborah Solomon, she said.

Logan moaned. I love her! he said.

She's a writer with *The New York Times,* said Thebes.

Logan's arm slipped off the bed and he picked up a Public Enemy CD that was lying on the floor and held it to his face.

He thinks that's Deborah Solomon, whispered Thebes.

Logan was out. Thebes hustled off to her bedroom,

took a running jump from the doorway and landed on her bed. Righteous air, I said. Sweet dreams.

I went downstairs and cleaned up the Cascade and then headed back up to make sure Logan was still breathing and hadn't choked on his own vomit. He was fine, snoring softly, hadn't moved at all. But I could hear Thebes crying. I went into her room and sat down beside her on the bed. Hey, I said. She was hiding her face behind a book. What's up, buttercup? I asked. She couldn't talk. I gently pulled the book away from her face so I could have a look at her. I smiled. She was a mess. I put her book down on the floor and held her and sang a few lame songs and told her Min was going to pull through, she always does, she's strong. She's so strong.

Thebes told me she'd stuck her arm in a machine at Pharma Plus and found out that her blood pressure is high but not dangerously high.

High's the new normal around here, I think, I told her. I rocked her like a baby. I sang every lullaby I knew, and some old Talking Heads and even some George Clinton. She told me I'd lost her place in her *Quidditch Through the Ages* book but it was okay. Eventually she fell asleep in my arms.

That night I had a dream that Min had showered, and the kids and I had thrown a party. Hundreds of people showed up, people from around the world. Logan was in charge of the music and Thebes poured the champagne. Even Cherkis showed up, but he stayed in the yard and the kids scampered in and out of the house bringing him stuff and exchanging furtive messages.

Thebes was all business in the morning, running around the house getting her school stuff together, talking non-stop. Every so often she'd inhale sharply like she really needed an infusion of air right then to get her through her next story. It reminded me of Min and how she used to demonstrate her hyperventilating technique. Her goal had been to pass out in our tree house and then "accidentally" fall out of the tree to her death.

Thebes was still wearing her blue terry cloth outfit, but she'd washed her face and combed her hair a bit, on the sides, in the front. I was still stretched out in her little bed going, Mmmm-hmmmm, mmmm-hmmmm, really, yeah, wow, mmmm-hmmmmm, while she motored around the place getting ready.

You know what I hate? she said.

No, what.

When my teacher uses *carpet* as a verb, she said. She put on her teacher voice. We're carpeting. After carpet I'll help you work out your personal problems. When we car-pet we keep our hands in our laps.

What's carpeting? I asked.

We sit on a carpet and talk, said Thebes.

That sounds nice, I said.

Show me ten! said Thebes.

What? I asked.

My teacher says that all the time, she said. It means

show me ten fingers, like show me your hands so I know you're not fooling around with them during carpet. I told Thebes that the next time her teacher asks them to show her ten, she should say she's only got two, and hold up her middle fingers.

Uh, no, said Thebes. She stopped shoving things into her backpack long enough to give me a look. First of all, she told me, eleven-year-olds at her school don't do that, yet. Well, not the girls. And second, she already was not enjoying a lot of status at school, partly because of her prodigious kung fu skills that she couldn't help, and partly because of her habit of knocking herself in the head in a vain attempt to dislodge the fragment of scalpel stuck inside. I'm on thin ice in the social hierarchy department, she told me. I'm not exactly a popular girl.

Hey, but, I said, where do you think it would go?

Where what would go? she said.

The scalpel, I said, like if you did manage to dislodge it. I mean, it would still be stuck in your head, right?

Yeah, she said, but not in my brain. It would be somewhere between my brain and my skull, in that nook, and then it would be a simple laser procedure or something like that to remove it.

Where's Logan? I asked her. She didn't know. He'd left already. Oh, okay, I said. Does he often come home drunk?

No, said Thebes. That was an aberration. Then she started talking about her commemorative-plate project. She had to glue things onto a paper plate, things that had sort of defined her world in the last year. Her teacher had told her that she couldn't glue on pictures of the World Trade Center towers.

Why can't you? I asked her.

Because, said Thebes, that didn't involve me personally.

Well, I said, but in a broader sense, yeah, it did . . .

Other kids, said Thebes, have Stomp ticket stubs and birthday cake candles and photo-booth pictures, things like that, and now I have to start all over again.

Hey, I said, why don't you put some of your lyrics on the plate. That would be cool.

On my plate? said Thebes. Which will be pinned up in public along the blackboard with all the others? Are you *insane?* Like that wouldn't totally clinch my status as top dork of the universe. Are you going to stay in bed all day? She frowned.

No, I said. Definitely not. We have to get ready.

She came over and put her hands on my legs and her face close to mine. I'll flip you later, she told me. You'll love it.

Hey, I said, really, your lyrics are beautiful, you know.

No, they're embarrassing, she said.

Why? I asked her. I told her that I wrote sometimes. Poems or short stories, I said, whatever, if I'm feeling . . . you know . . .

Thebes looked at me like I'd just admitted to occasionally starting grease fires at old folks homes or something, just every once in a while, just to make sense of my world. Hmmm, yeah, she said. Well, what are they about? she asked. Wait! Let me guess! Sex and death?

And love, I told her.

Sick, she said. She told me that tonight she had to start working on her "Helping the United Nations Rid the World of Racial Discrimination" speech and read an entire book for the read-a-thon to raise funds for the children of some Vietnamese province.

Holy shit, I said, and lay down again. Can I just give you twenty bucks? Like, who would know if you'd read the book or not?

She said no, that would be cheating.

I'll be home at 3:45 precisely, she said. Shalom. She waved from the hall and left. I stared at the ceiling. She returned.

Hey! she said.

Yeah?

Did you know that I've been banned from Zellers for two years for having a perfume testers war with my friends?

No, I said, that's funny.

That I have friends? said Thebes.

No! I said.

Just kidding, she said. I had a mug shot taken, she told me. They had those measuring lines and everything. That's why my hair is purple now. I dyed it after they took my photo so I can still cut through Zellers undercover on my way to school.

Okay, I said. See ya later.

Not if I see you first, said Thebes. Psych. She left. She came back again.

Thebes, I said, you're killing me. She asked me if I was going to see Min today.

Yeah, I said.

Tell her I love her, said Thebes. Hug her and kiss her for me. But gently.

I will, I said.

Remind her of the singing orange on the patio at Hermosa Beach, said Thebes.

Okay, I will, I said.

I had this singing orange, said Thebes, you know? And it killed Min. I had like this face on it—oh craps! Thebes had just looked at her clock radio, next to the bed. She said she had to go or she'd get "written up" and she could not afford a third "death note" or . . . She grabbed her throat and pretended to choke herself.

You should really go, Thebie, I said.

Okay, but one last thing? she said. Are you serious about trying to find Cherkis?

Yeah, I am, I said.

High-five, said Thebes.

I got up and went to Logan's room and knocked on the door. There was a tiny tag from the dry cleaners stuck to the door that said "Press Only." No answer. I knocked again. Logan? I said. I opened the door.

Empty room. I walked over to his desk. He'd carved the words *Are You a Ghost?* into a jagged heart. And had also written in black ink the words *It's Official. That grade 12 girl is now more imagination than reality. Shitty.* And also: *Hey, there, even if you do get your braces off, there's still nothing the orthodontist can do about your sad, sad eyes.* And next to his computer he'd written a message to himself: *No, you will not type the letters you believe make up your father's name into that small rectangle. Don't be a loser.* And beneath that, he'd carved a rough drawing of the planet Earth and inside it the words: *No one can stay.*

Okay. I went downstairs and looked around. Messy. Grey light. Dust everywhere. Piles of books and clothes. Dirty dishes in the kitchen. Crumbs. Old newspapers. No problem. I sent a telepathic message to Marc. I hope you're having a blast at your ashram. I put on one of Logan's CDs and started cleaning up. There were small though emphatic stick-it notes all over the kitchen. *Cups! Glasses! Coffee off! I love you, Min! No more fires! Don't forget your vitamin B stress therapy! You're the best!* All in Thebie's loopy handwriting.

The phone rang and I picked it up and said hello. It was the secretary at Logan's school. Logan hadn't shown up for his first class. He's got a doctor's appointment, I said. That was all right, they said, but next time I should let them know first thing in the morning. Done and done! I said. I appreciate your call. I hung up. Was I supposed to find him? I finished cleaning up and went into the backyard for a smoke.

The next-door neighbour came out, a big guy in a yellow Haile Selassie T-shirt. Hey, I said. How's it going?

Not bad, he said, but it'd be better if you guys weren't throwing hatchets into my yard all night.

Oh, yeah, I said. Yeahhh . . . it won't happen again.

No, it won't, he said. Because I've got them all over here and I'm not giving them back.

Oh, I said, all right. Freaking uptight guy considering the shirt he's got on, I thought. And there's got to be a hatchet store around here where I could get reinforcements.

Who are you, anyway? he asked.

I'm Hattie, Min's sister. I'm visiting.

Yeah? he said.

Yeah, I said.

You don't look anything like her, he said.

I've had a lot of work done, I said. I stared off into space, hoping he'd disappear.

Hey, I don't mean to be rude, he said, but your sister there, Min, what's up with her? What's her deal?

Min's cool, I said. There's no deal. I got up and went into the house and watched from a window as he and his man Selassie walked away. Then I went back out and sat down on the deck. There was a Ping-Pong table in the centre of the yard, and behind it, up against the yellow fence, a purple playhouse plastered with stencils of frogs and cars and suns and lizards. Three bikes were chained to a tree. There was a little dilapidated shack that had once been Min's studio, and a fire pit piled with charred logs. I noticed two birdhouses up high in a tree, one painted with pink and purple hearts and the other with orange flames and streaks of dripping blood against a black background. Min had told me about the kids' birdhouses, how she'd climbed the tree in a dust storm and nailed them to a branch.

Everything in life, except her kids, made her impatient. She had tried to do a million things. She'd wanted to be a documentary filmmaker and then a painter and then

a tiny-ceramic-figure maker. None of it panned out. She'd
be full of enthusiasm at first, full of big ideas and energy
and drive, but it would all gradually evaporate and disappear. She could never maintain the momentum or the
concentration or the confidence she needed to get anything done. She'd fight with the people who were helping
her get set up or she'd hate what she had created and
destroy it in a spectacular way or she'd get it into her head
that everything was so damn futile, anyway, why bother,
what's the point, what difference does it make. And then
she'd go to bed for four months. Cherkis was supportive
at first; he believed in her abilities and he loved her. He'd
run around trying to get the supplies she needed, setting
up a darkroom in the house, building the heated studio in
the backyard, making the meals, cleaning the house, doing
the shopping, while she attacked yet another project with
gusto and then threw her arms in the air and shit-canned
it for something else . . . or nothing.

I threw my cigarette into the pit and went back
inside. The phone rang again. It was the hospital.

Who am I speaking with?

Uh, Hattie?

Are you family?

Yeah.

Logan was staging some sort of sit-in in the waiting
room, refusing to leave until he saw his mom, and they
were wondering if I would come and get him.

I had to call a cab again because Logan had taken the
van. When I got there he was lying on his back in the
grass outside the front entrance of the hospital. I guessed

they had managed to kick him out of the waiting room. There was a plastic Safeway bag next to him. I pulled the headphone off one of his ears.

What are you doing? I asked him.

What are you doing? he asked me.

They called and said you weren't going to leave until you saw Min. And you missed your first class. The school called too. And the neighbour guy is keeping your hatchets *and* you shouldn't take the van if you don't have a licence. Plus you were really drunk last night and Thebes and I had to put you to bed. Is this all normal or what? I've been here like seventeen hours. I sat down beside him on the grass.

I have some stuff for her and I wanted to give it to her, that's it, he said.

What stuff?

Yogourt and some other stuff, he said. We decided to try going back in. We took the elevator to the sixth floor and banged on the locked glass doors to the psych ward. A nurse buzzed us in but with the very least amount of enthusiasm I have ever witnessed within the helping profession. She might have been brandishing a switchblade behind her stacks of patient folders.

Yes? she said.

Hi, I said. My name is Hattie Troutman. I'm Min's sister. And this is Logan, her son. We were here yesterday when she was admitted and Logan would really like to give her a few things. They're not flammable or sharp.

Visiting hours begin at 4 p.m., she said.

I know, I said. And then didn't know what to say after

that. I know, I said again. But can you make an exception just this once? He's come all the way out here. He's got yogourt and—

We provide our patients with meals, she said. We don't need family to bring food from outside.

Yeah, I know, but—

You can leave the bag with me and I'll give it to the patient after rounds. Logan started walking down the hall towards Min's room. Excuse me! said the nurse.

He deked into Min's room and disappeared, and the nurse got up from behind her files and flew after him. Bernie, the "good stuff" guy, saw her running and got up from his desk and followed her, and I followed him. Logan was sitting in a chair next to Min's bed. He was hunched over her and wiping away tears with the rim of his hood. Min was asleep or looked that way anyway. Jeanette, her bald roommate, was there too, standing next to Logan and gently rubbing his back. She was still wearing her Superman T-shirt and her dark shades but this time she was also wearing pants.

Hey, buddy, she whispered. She took really deep, loud breaths. Hey, buddy. Things will work out.

She was a crazy, institutionalized superhero but still she was probably somewhat correct, and I was touched by her concern. Bernie and the nurse talked about their strict policies and the need to respect those policies and a bunch of other things that I wasn't really listening to, although I repeatedly told them that I understood. I asked Bernie if I could speak to Min for a minute alone. Logan said he'd go back to the waiting room.

I put my face close to Min's and told her again that I loved her. I told her what I had told her so many times when we were kids. You'll be fine, I said, you'll get better. I promise.

She opened her eyes and looked at me, but she didn't say anything and she didn't smile.

I told her I'd be right back. I just wanted to talk to her doctor for a minute. As I walked towards the door I heard her whisper my name, so I went back to her bed and said, Yeah? And she asked me please not to come back.

What? I said.

She mouthed the word *sorry* and then closed her eyes, and I just stood there staring at her.

But, Min, I said, I want to see you. That's why I'm here. I want to be with you.

She opened her eyes again and whispered, No, Hattie, please don't come back here. And don't bring the kids, it's too hard.

And that was it for her, no more talking, so I left.

I told Bernie I wanted to talk to Min's doctor. He said Min's doctor was busy with other patients at the moment. I told him I'd wait. Logan slowly, silently raised his middle finger to Bernie's back and said, Good stuff, as Bernie walked away.

Hey, don't, I said. I told Logan to take the van and go to school. Oh, and if anybody asked, to say he'd had a doctor's appointment. Keep our stories straight. I'd get the scoop on Min and meet him at home.

I thought you didn't want me driving without a licence, he said.

Yeah, I know, I said, but just be careful. Stay in your lane, don't speed. Take your hood off. I reached out to pull it down, but he moved his head back and smiled.

Don't, he said.

Keep the music down, too, I said.

Fine, said Logan. He bent over, reached under his chair and grabbed his basketball. He spun it on one finger and then threw it against the wall, against a What is Schizophrenia poster, caught it again, yanked his headphones up around his ears, and slid on out of there. The nurse behind the desk reminded Logan that this was a quiet zone, and he threw his ball gently against the elevator down-button. The doors opened, and he disappeared.

Min's doctor told me that she was psychotic, entirely out of touch with reality, and it wouldn't make any difference to her if she had visitors or not. It makes the family feel better when they visit but it does nothing for the patient, he said. In fact, I've found it distresses the patient more.

Are you sure? I asked him.

Uh, yes, he said, I'm quite sure. Anything else? he asked.

How long will she be here? I said.

Hard to say, he said. As soon as she begins to participate in her own care we'll have something to talk about. But that seems a ways off.

I imagined a nice long, fireside chat with this guy. There were so many things I wanted to ask him, but he had torpedoes to issue and other brains to jump-start

and he'd given me enough face time. He smiled awkwardly, tapped his pen on his chart twice and began to
walk away. I grabbed his arm and said, hey, thank you,
have a great day, I'm sorry, and then he was gone.

When I got back to the house, Logan was there watching
TV. And school? I asked him. I held out my hands.

Expelled, he said. You're supposed to call them.

What? I said. What are you talking about?

Call them, he said. He stared at the TV. I could still
make out the words *Deborah Solomon, be my girlfriend* written
in the dust on the screen.

You tell me, I said. I sat down next to him and put
my arm around his shoulders. He flinched but he didn't
move away. I stared at the TV with him. What do you
like so much about Deborah Solomon? I asked him. He
shrugged. No, really? The older woman thing? I asked.

No, he said.

What, then?

I don't know, he said.

Well, what? I asked again.

She's solid, he said, finally. And she doesn't back away
from shit.

So why were you expelled? I asked.

It was just . . . nothing, he said.

You got expelled for nothing? Like, your principal
just pulls random names out of a hat.

Logan sighed. I felt his shoulder rise and collapse.
Okay, he said. And then we had this conversation.

Logan: I was shooting hoops with this kid whose
    older brother is with The Deuce.

Me: Really?

Logan: Yeah.

Me: Oh. So. Hmm.

Logan: Yeah.

Me: Okay, so how was it?

Logan: Do you even know what The Deuce is?

Me: No. A gang?

Logan: Yeah. So did you know their colour is
    baby blue?

Me: Oh, that's perfect.

Logan: What do you mean?

Me: The irony of it.

Logan: No. It's just their colour.

Me: Well, it's a nice one.

Logan: And the kid I was shooting hoops with
    was wearing a baby blue shirt.

Me: I thought colours weren't allowed at your
    school.

Logan: Well, you can't . . . it's just a colour. You
    can't really ban a—

Me: No, but, you know, explicit gang colours.

Logan: No.

Me: Okay, you'd know.

Logan: So, we're there and—

Me: School property?

Logan: Yeah. Don't say "school property." I hate
    that expression.

Me: Okay.

Logan: We're there and these guys come up to
     where we are, only I'm off a bit, a little away
     from them, and these guys are talking to the
     kid I'm playing with.

Me: Yeah?

Logan: And then he goes off a bit with them,
     over to the side, by the wall.

Me: Uh-huh.

Logan: And I can't really hear what they're
     saying or anything, but then a few minutes
     later he comes back and he tells me they
     took his shirt.

Me: The baby blue one?

Logan: Yeah, he had another one under it.

Me: Oh, that's good.

Logan: And his Walkman.

Me: Poor kid. All calm, just like that?

Logan: Yeah.

Me: Well, that's scary. Did you go report it?

Logan: (Doesn't say anything, just looks at me
     for a second.)

Me: What?

Logan: Okay. Hattie. This kid said they were I.P.

Me: So?

Logan: You don't go to the principal's office and
     say you just got robbed by the Posse.

Me: No? You don't?

Logan: Okay. Hattie. What do you think would
     happen?

Me: I don't know.

Logan: Yeah. Nothing. They don't go to school.

Me: Well, he could phone the cops.

Logan: No.

Me: Well, I would.

Logan: No.

Me: No?

Logan: So then this kid said that they had a knife.

Me: Oh my god.

Logan: And then the kid said, Well, at least they didn't see this.

Me: See what?

Logan: His binder.

Me: What would the I.P. do with a binder?

Logan: 'Cause it said "Posse Killers" on it.

Me: Oh my god. That kid is a deuce?

Logan: Not "a deuce." *Deuce*.

Me: That kid's Deuce?

Logan: No, that doesn't sound right either.

Me: How about, is that kid a member of The Deuce?

Logan: Okay. No. But his older brother is.

Me: Okay. But, you know, I'm concerned that—

Logan: But this kid used to be in The Deuce.

Me: Really?

Logan: He just got out of jail.

Me: What? Seriously? You're playing basketball with gangsters who've been in prison?

Logan: He's a nice guy, though.

Me: Well, god, listen, Logan—

Logan: He's trying to get his shit together.

Me: Hmmm. Well . . .

Logan: So anyway, I go back inside and like five
minutes later on the P.A. it's like, Logan
Troutman, would you please come to the
office, so I go and they say, Oh, we saw you
playing basketball with certain individuals
known to have gang ties and we've already
warned you about this blahblahblah, and I'm
like, So? I had a spare. And they're like, That's
three strikes, you're out. Lame.

Me: Really.

Logan: Mmm-hmmm.

Me: But like how were you technically supposed
to know that they were in a gang? Or gangs,
plural, whatever.

Logan: They obviously know I know.

Me: Oh.

I didn't know exactly what he meant, but it seemed like
we'd exhausted that point and it didn't matter anyway.

We're hitting the road, I said.

What road? he said.

You, me, Thebie, we're going on a road trip, I said.
We're gonna look for Cherkis.

Logan stared at the TV like it was the only thing
standing between him and eternal happiness. Like a
retriever stares at a squirrel before all hell breaks loose.
Then he loosened up.

Where? he asked.

I don't know, I said. South Dakota . . . I'm not sure. I have one lead.

What do we do if we find him?

I don't know, I said.

What do we do if we don't find him?

I don't know that, either, I said.

Awesome, he said. But why?

I didn't know if he was being sarcastic or not. Min wants us to, I said. It was her idea.

Really? said Logan. She never even talks about him.

I know, I said, but I think she understands now that she needs his help. We can phone her from the road.

I don't know, said Logan.

What don't you know? I asked.

Logan got up and walked to the kitchen.

I phoned the hospital again and asked to speak to Min. The nurse told me that Min did not want to talk to me. I know, I said, but I don't think she means it.

She'd prefer not to see you, said the nurse.

What about her kids? I said.

Min doesn't want any visitors, said the nurse.

I wasn't surprised. I had refused to help her die and her kids reminded her of important reasons to live. She had done this before when she was deeply psychotic, turned her back, flipped us the bird, walked away. My parents once drove for days to the West Coast trying to find out where she'd disappeared to and when they got to her apartment she refused to open the door and then called the cops to say they were harassing her. There had been so many times that she told me never to call her again. I would come all the way from Paris to see her and she'd tell me to go to hell. I love you, Hattie, she'd say, but please go away. At first I was hurt and mystified. One time I waited all night in minus-twenty weather outside her front door, begging her to open it and let me in. I'd spent hours, days, following her around town, trying to get her to talk to me, to acknowledge me, to realize that all I wanted to do was help her. She phoned the cops and told them I was stalking her. I was used to it now. I understood. She would eventually change her mind, let me back into her life, and the temporary banishment would never be spoken of.

But this was the first time she'd refused to see her kids.

Logan came back into the living room and sat down on the couch. What don't you know? I asked him again. He said he didn't know. You don't know what you don't know? I said.

Well, he said, I'd kind of like not to be interrogated. I know that.

Do you mean you don't know if we should be leaving Min? I asked him.

I don't know, he said.

We're obviously coming back, though, I said. I mean, you know, obviously.

I know, yeah, he said. Obviously.

But you just don't know, I said.

Yeah.

Yeah . . . but I kind of know, I said.

No, you don't, he said. But it doesn't matter. He smiled sympathetically, then picked up a magazine and started to read.

four

I WANTED US TO PACK EVERYTHING UP, load the
van, lock up the house, get maps, all that stuff, and then
pick up Thebes at school on our way out of town. But
Logan said no, Thebes would want to pack her own stuff,
she had weird habits and needed weird things with her at
all times. So we did everything we could without packing
her stuff and then Logan moved some of the furniture

and tried to teach me how to do a pick-and-roll and some other basketball manoeuvres for a few hours (Like this? No, no. Like this? No, no. Like this? No, no.) while we waited for her to get home.

Bonjourno! she said when she finally arrived, her trademark greeting, apparently. She dropped her backpack on the kitchen floor and bolted for the remote before Logan could get it.

Theodora! I said. Welcome home, pack your stuff, we're leaving.

How do you spell *peyote*? asked Logan. He was making a list of supplies we'd have to pick up before we left.

N-O, I said.

Okay, I have to phone Abbey and cancel rehearsals, said Thebes.

If, along the way, something is gained, then something will also be lost. Those words had been emblazoned on Min's bedroom wall, burned into the wallpaper with a charred wine-bottle cork. Our parents dismissed them as pseudo-profound, angsty-adolescent babble, but they haunted me. Why should that be? I wondered. How did she know that? Did she really believe it, or did she just like the way those words looked in burnt cork?

I heard the universe answering back in the form of the wind and the sun and the earth's orbit and the ocean's tide and the world's wild rivers and the nomadic peoples of Outer Mongolia . . . Things move, Hattie. Perpetual motion. Dig it or die . . . You've got a crumb on your lip.

Actually, that was Marc I was hearing on our last day in Paris as he explained to me exactly why he really needed to morph from a tangible boyfriend into a painful memory.

But couldn't I move with you? I also enjoy the sensations of motion, I told him. I flapped my arms around and did a little dance in my petite wrought-iron chair. *Do not ever return to this café*, I told myself.

Marc said it was important for us to detach, to stand alone, to experience ourselves, to answer to our inner something, to recognize the divinity that resides within each of us.

But what if our in-house divinities are telling us exactly the same thing? I asked him. Like, how many ideas are out there, anyway? Ours may match.

Hattie, said Marc, be well. Find your centre. Be happy. Stand alone for a while and see what it's like.

I asked him if I could get away with *lying down* alone for a while instead, like maybe on a desolate stretch of railroad. He smiled and hugged me. Love is the answer, he said.

To what? I asked him.

Everything! he said.

Cool, cool, I said.

He asked me if I could maybe get the cheque because he'd already changed all his euros into rupees.

You have to phone my school, said Logan. He was sitting on the floor surrounded by a mountain range of CDs that he was organizing for the trip.

Why? I asked him. You're expelled. What's to say?

They want to know that you know, said Logan.

Let me! said Thebes. I'm good at being Min. Logan slid the phone across the floor.

Yes, she said, my name is Min Troutman and I'm—Min Troutman. Yeah. *T-R-O-U-T-M-A-N*. And I'm—Min. Yeah, Min. *M-I-N*.

I'm his mother.

Yeah, totally! Full-time job, eh?

That's not how Min talks, I whispered to Logan.

He shrugged.

Thebes, I said, give me the phone. She turned her back to me and kept on talking.

What? said Thebes. Oh. Logan. Troutman . . . *T-R-O-U-T-M-A-N* . . . What? . . . Yo! Logan! He goes to that school! Don't you know his name? Logan! . . . *L-O-G-A-N!*

Thebes, I said. Give me the phone right now.

It's a big school? said Thebes. Well, then, you'll be happy to be rid of one, eh?

Logan and I were trying not to laugh. I held out my hand for the phone.

I know it's serious, right! said Thebes. This kid is driving me crazy, trust me. We're taking him to a, like a, like an al-Qaeda training camp, but not really. It's one of those boot camps for—

I grabbed the phone out of her hand and said hello. There was silence on the other end. Whoever Thebes had been talking to had hung up. Should I call back? I asked Logan.

No, don't bother, he said, it won't make any difference. They'll figure it out.

I called Thebes's school and told the secretary that we were going on a road trip so Thebes wouldn't be there for a week or so. The woman said Thebes was a great student and it wouldn't make any difference.

Is this Min? asked the woman.

No, I said. This is Min's sister.

Oh, said the woman, is everything okay at home?

Mostly, I said. More or less. The woman said she hoped we had a great time. Well, thank you! I said.

Yeah, um . . . , she said.

Is there a problem? I asked her.

No, no, no, she said, there's not a problem. It's just that Thebes, you know . . . well, she regrets being born.

What? I said. What do you mean?

She said it again, today, said the woman.

Today? I thought. After her hyper, jazzed-up start in the morning?

She doesn't want anybody to know, said the woman. Particularly her mother. She doesn't want to worry her.

Yeah, I said.

The woman asked me if I knew that Thebes had written something on the girls' bathroom wall in indelible ink.

No, I said, I didn't know that. I looked at Thebes. She was stuffing coloured construction paper into a backpack. What did she write? I whispered.

The woman said Thebes had written, *Wanna do a walk-around in dreamtime, gonna seek my old bush soul.*

That's what she wrote on the bathroom wall?

Mmmm, yeah, said the woman. She had to paint over it because the custodian couldn't get it off with soap.

Okay, I said, well, thanks for letting me know. Thebes had finished filling her backpack with paper and was drawing something on her foot. I hung up and told Thebes that everything was cool at her school. They'll miss you, though, I said.

Oh, they don't care, Thebes said. We don't do anything in June anyway except clean up and have talking circles and go on lame field trips to the mint and I always have to be partners with Rajbeer because he's new and shy and my teacher pretends that he needs me instead of admitting the truth, which is that nobody else wants to be my partner. I don't even think Rajbeer wants to be my partner but he's forced to be. He doesn't even think I'm a person.

Logan put his arm around Thebes. It's not easy being a girl, he said. Like you, he added.

True dat, my brotha, said Thebes. She stopped drawing on her foot and wrapped her arms around his skinny waist.

But, Thebie, he said, just remember you're a little white kid. He rubbed her matted purple head. She snapped the elastic waistband of his boxers, which were foaming out around the top of his XXX pants. You don't always have to talk like Chuck D, or whatever. In fact, I really wish you wouldn't, especially on the road, like, in America. 'Cause that'll be really embarrassing.

Dawg, said Thebes, I gotta—

Seriously, Thebie. You have to stop doing that.

Oh, fine, said Thebes. She looked tired, a little deflated.

———

I sat at the dining room table and drew a map of the universe as I knew it at that precise moment. The planet of Min, the planet of Cherkis, the stars of Thebes and Logan, vast and perilous milky distances in between. Enemy space stations in the form of foster homes and me as a UFO. Min didn't want to see her kids. Min didn't want to see me. Her kids wanted nothing more than to be with her. I wanted my sister back. Cherkis had wanted to be with his kids but Min had sent him packing. Min says she'll kill herself if Cherkis takes the kids but now she seems to want to die anyway.

The phone rang. Thebie answered it. Bonjourno! she said. Oh yeah, hang on. It's for you, loser, she said. She slid the phone along the floor to Logan.

Oh hey, he said, all tender. He tried to lower his voice. How's it going? Oh yeah, sorry about that, I was gonna but uh . . . what? I know. Yeah, he said into the phone, I'm really sorry. I was going to, but . . . what? Thebie threw an empty Coke can at Logan. Yeah, he said. Did you get that colour you wanted? Logan threw the can back at Thebie and missed. Yeah? I bet it looks good. Yeah? That's nice.

It's a girl, Thebie told me. She pretended she was kissing someone and then she started hugging herself and moving around like she was dancing. Logan turned his back on her.

How many washes before it comes out? he asked. Yeah? Oh, nice. Yeah, I will. I promise. Okay. Take it easy. He hung up.

Thebes, you're a fucking retard, he said.

Who was that? I asked. Deborah Solomon?

Yeah, he said.

It was this girl who wears a Batman sheet as a dress and rides an old-lady bike, said Thebes. Min says she's *besotted* with Logan. Sounds like a bedwetter. She's emo.

Shut up, said Logan.

You didn't tell her you were going to be gone for a while? I said.

Nah, it was too hard to explain, he said. Plus, we're supposed to be in a cooling-off period.

We loaded all our stuff into the van and left. On the way out of town we dropped the invisible plecostomas off at one of Thebes's friends. I had no idea what Thebes had packed but her suitcase was bulging and she had various backpacks filled with other stuff and a big cardboard box of art supplies.

Should we stop at the hospital and say goodbye to Min? asked Thebes.

No, I said. She'll be okay. She's getting better. We'll call her from the road. I couldn't guarantee that Min would answer the call, probably not, considering she'd just said she didn't want to see or talk to us. Thebes seemed satisfied.

Word, she said. Logan looked at her. What? she said.

Logan would have the front seat for the first hour and then it would be Thebes's turn. We'd take turns playing our CDs and Logan would keep track of whose turn it was. He was not allowed to drive. We were heading south towards the border, and then we'd stop and figure things out from there.

On the way out of town we saw this guy standing by the side of the highway holding up a sign that said There are Three Eternal Destinies. And beneath it was a web address. Logan wondered if the guy was real. Let's see if he moves, he said. He pretended to grab the steering wheel and I yelled at him not to do that and he apologized and then I apologized for yelling and he said it was okay, Min never yelled any more and it kind of made him feel more normal to be yelled at every once in a while.

Let's remember that website, said Thebes. I want to find out which of those three eternal destinies is mine. She crawled into the back seat to get some of her art supplies. She was back there for a while. I thought maybe she'd fallen asleep. But then she popped her head up and passed me a piece of paper with some writing on it. It said:

In Scrabble you've got a certain amount of time to make sense of your randomly picked letters, to make words, not necessarily to know what they mean, but to score points, to bluff, to bingo, to win.

What is this? I asked her.

Grandma's last words, she said. I write them down at least once a week so I don't forget them.

I wasn't sure that those were, in fact, my mother's last words. I'd been with her when she died, and just before she slipped into unconsciousness she held my hand and told me that whatever happened, I was not responsible for saving Min. But did she mean it or was dying similar to Scrabble in that you had a finite amount of time to bluff. My mother was an eternal optimist when it came to Min. Every few months she'd come up with some new diagnosis, one she'd make on her own with help from library books, and new hope for Min's recovery. Our own family doctor had given up on Min. He said there was nothing wrong with her that a little maturity wouldn't straighten out. She needed to grow up, basically, was his theory.

We talked for a while about Grandma, how she'd once been rescued at sea and dragged onto some Jamaican beach by a group of fishermen. She had taken Thebes to Jamaica for a short holiday after her brain surgery and they'd gone banana boating. My mother fell off and was laughing so hard she couldn't climb back onto the boat.

She was also really fat, said Thebes.

So a bunch of guys saw her laughing and bobbing way out in the sea and swam out to rescue her.

One guy on each extremity, said Thebes. Grandma looked like a starfish, a laughing starfish. Even though salt water was splashing into her mouth, she couldn't stop laughing, said Thebes.

Yeah, I said, remember when she was almost trampled to death by that herd of elephants?

Yeah, said Thebes. At the last second some Kenyan shepherd yanked her out of the way.

Hmm, I said, she liked to travel around the world getting into trouble and being rescued. In that way she was a little like Min. In that way she was a little like all of us. Once, I mentioned off-handedly to her that I was sometimes afraid of Min, that I wished I didn't have to share a room with her because I was tired of staying up late, night after night, waiting for Min to fall asleep first so I wouldn't have to worry about her stabbing me in my sleep. I'd kind of been kidding, but I'd wanted my mother to know that although I was young, and although I loved my sister, and although I *usually* trusted her, I didn't *always* trust her. My mother scooped me up in her arms and laughed and said I didn't have to worry, really, Min was only a danger, and a slight danger at that, to herself. I hadn't known exactly how that was supposed to be reassuring. I put bubble wrap on the floor around my bed, just in case, so I'd be able to hear it popping if she walked towards me late at night with a butcher knife in her hand. Nothing that crazy ever did happen.

We were zipping along the highway towards the U.S. border. Not a single cloud in the sky, just a jet stream that resembled arthritic vertebrae and a few bossy crows swooping around up high, plotting some sort of attack. We were quiet now, for about six seconds, staring out the windows of the van in three different directions.

Then Thebes said, Min told me a story about you.

Yeah? I said.

About you guys renting scooters in Corfu and riding on a road that circled and circled and rose and rose until you were finally at the highest peak of the island, said

Thebes. Nothing but blue sky, rock and sea. Kids threw pomegranates at you and old men laughed. On the way back down you took a turn too sharply and wiped out and scraped layers of skin off your legs.

We had such a hard time getting off that island, I said. Our parents had paid for that trip after one of Min's meltdowns. Logan was just a baby and Cherkis took care of him while we were gone. Cherkis brought us to the airport and waved to us from the observation deck with Logan all curled up against his chest in a Snugli.

Why? Weren't there boats? asked Thebes.

Well, yeah, I said, but the one we wanted to take left every morning at six and we could never get up on time. That went on for days.

Well, did you have an alarm clock, like a tiny travel one? she asked.

No, we didn't have anything at all, I said. We were counting on the sun.

That's flaky. What about a rooster? Did you have any roosters?

No. Just the sun. If we'd had a rooster, we'd have eaten it.

Well, why didn't you stay up all night? she asked.

We tried that, I said.

And?

And it didn't work either, I said. We couldn't stay up past three or four.

Why not?

I don't know. We were so baked from the sun and probably dehydrated and malnourished.

Oh, said Thebes.

Logan's chin clunked onto his chest and then snapped back up, then down again. He was out.

Hey, let's draw on him, said Thebes. She was waving around a Sharpie.

No, don't, I said.

I'll put *666* on his forehead.

No, don't, I said again.

But eventually you got off the island, she said.

Yeah, I said, so then finally, there was this guy, his name was Pantilas, I think, something like that, and he hated us, so he told us he'd make sure to get us to the boat on time.

Why did he hate you?

Because we were terrible olive pickers, I said. We tried to work for him.

Nothing you guys did worked out! she said.

I adjusted my rear-view mirror and considered my current plan. Min had told me that at one point Cherkis was the curator of an art gallery in the middle of a field somewhere outside Murdo, South Dakota. It was an old, abandoned farmhouse. Cherkis had crammed all his art onto the main floor and was living in the second storey and the attic. He had taken a lot of blurry photographs. Min had once told me that Cherkis's life's work had been, maybe still was, to create the perfect level of pixel breakdown without compromising the essence of the image. He didn't feel right about charging admission and hated the idea of advertising, plus nobody really showed up anyway, where the hell is Murdo, let alone a field outside of it, let alone a dilapidated farmhouse/gallery, so eventually, actually really quickly, he went broke. But that's where we were going. Point A.

So, Murdo, eh? said Thebes.

Yeah, I said. He won't be there, but maybe there'll be someone who knows where he went.

He used to balance me on his face when I was a baby, and he tie-dyed all my onesies, said Thebes. Min told me.

Logan remembered smashing into a tree while trying to show off his flashing runners and Cherkis carrying him eight or nine blocks all the way to the hospital. They were both covered in Logan's blood. Cherkis held him down while the Emergency staff stitched up Logan's head, then he returned his kid intact to Min, and, with streaks of blood still on his face, left town in a silver rental car loaded with options.

five

I'D FORGOTTEN ABOUT THE BORDER. Logan had dozed off again. I yanked on his hoodie and told him to wake up.

What the *F,* he said. Where are we?

Checkpoint Charlie, said Thebes. Act natural. We cruised past the wanky little "tuck stand," as Logan called our Canada Customs building. Nobody was coming into

Canada, the guy inside the cracked booth looked like he was busy counting his ribs or something, and we pulled up to the shiny space-station Star Wars thing on the American side.

Don't say anything, Thebie, I mean it, I said to her.

Geez Louise! she said. Bust a cap in my—

Seriously, keep your mouth shut. Please? I'll give you a dollar.

I will too, said Logan.

Thebes dropped out of sight and hit the floor of the van.

No, no, I said, don't lie on the floor, Thebie, they'll think we're kidnapping you. She popped up again, sat there in this ridiculously erect position, and mimed zipping up her lips and throwing away the key.

Hello, I said to the guy. How are you?

He ignored the question and asked me where we were from, where we were headed (family reunion in Minneapolis) and how long we'd be gone (forty-eight hours). These your kids? he asked.

No, they're my niece and nephew. They wanted to ride with me, uh, but their parents are going too. Flying. I stuck my arms out and made a whooshing sound that I'll regret all my life.

Is that true? the guy asked Logan.

Yeah.

This your aunt? he asked Thebes.

Nothing.

Hey there, darlin', said the guy, this your aunt?

Nothing.

Logan turned around and looked at her. I stared straight ahead into the great nation of America, waiting for the onset of dogs and AK-47s.

She doesn't talk, said Logan. Like, she can't. She's profoundly retarded.

The guy looked at me. She don't talk? he said.

Right, I said. She makes sounds sometimes but it's impossible to know what she means. I felt Thebie's foot through the back of my seat, gradually exerting pressure.

Her folks should get her checked out, said the guy.

Oh, I know, they have, but—

It's your guys' health care, right? he said. Socialism is really nice in theory but not when you've got a retarded kid that needs treatment, right?

I smiled. Yeah, exactly, I said.

It's too bad, he said. He looked at Thebes, shook his head.

I know, I said. Logan cleared his throat and started tapping the dashboard with his foot.

All right, said the guy, well, y'all have a good reunion. It's real sweet you're taking her with you.

Hey, yeah, I said. Thanks. She likes to travel.

Thebes picked up a book and lay down in the back seat. What are you reading? I asked her.

Corporate Media: Threat to Democracy, she said.

Thebes, man, said Logan, just say "this" and then hold up the book. God. Like you would actually say "Corporate Media: Threat to Democracy."

Well, she said, I don't date a girl who wets her bed.

She doesn't wet her bed, said Logan.

She wears Batman bedsheets, said Thebes.

Logan turned up the volume on his Discman and then stuck his head out the window like one of those stop signs that pops out of the side of a school bus. Thebes said that if she was eighteen and old enough to drink she'd start a book club.

We drove straight south into the heartland. Billboards told us not to abort our fetuses or to let our sins get us down or to worry about our bad credit and criminal records. For instant cash all we had to do was call a certain number. Bingo. Logan pulled his head back into the van and took a knife from his pocket.

What the hell is that? I asked him. A shiv?

Don't say "shiv," he said. He started to carve something into the dashboard.

Whoa, I said, stop that. He kept carving. Stop that! I said again.

What's he doing? asked Thebes. What's he doing? She was sucking on ice that she'd taken out of the cooler and water was dripping down her face and onto her terry cloth outfit. She took an ice cube out of her mouth and rubbed it on her forehead and then popped it back into her mouth. She was wearing a necklace with a huge, pear-sized plastic jewel dangling from it and a ring with an angel, arms outstretched.

Where'd you get that? I asked her.

Logan, she said. For Christmas.

My hands were shaking. We passed a lot of fields and

a few houses and a barn with giant words painted on the side. Bubba Where Are You, it said.

I miss Min, said Thebes. She leaned forward and put an arm around each of us.

I know, I said. I wanted to ask her why she regretted being born, if it was a knife-in-the-heart all-consuming regret or an intermittent, passing regret like a loose tooth you worry with your tongue every once in a while. I didn't know how to say the words. I didn't know how I'd answer her answer.

Why can't she be happy? asked Thebes.

She often is, I said. Life takes a long time. *What the hell does that mean, anyway?* Why would I say that to a kid who was already regretting being born?

Thebes sat back and tapped her Sharpie against her teeth. In the rear-view mirror I saw her squint against the setting sun like a desperado trying to get oriented. *Tap, tap, tap, tap, tap.* I was bracing myself for another question I wouldn't be able to answer. But she didn't ask it. Just kept knocking on her teeth with her marker and staring out at the darkening world. Logan had ignored my plea about not carving into the van and had written into the dash the words *Fear Yourself*.

Okay, that's it, we're stopping somewhere to eat, I said. This is what parents do when they're stumped, I thought. They feed their children.

Like what, said Logan, are we gonna graze in a field? I don't see any restaurants.

Sandwiches in the cooler, I said. Ham and cheese. There's fruit.

Awesome, he said. Budget.

We're not gonna eat in restaurants the whole time, I said. I had a wad of cash in my backpack that I hoped would get us through. I pulled into a rest stop next to a shitting chihuahua and two old RVers reading a newspaper at a picnic table.

We got out and walked around awhile, stretching our bodies, enjoying less proximity to each other, and I smoked a cigarette behind the women's can until Thebes caught me and told me I was going to get AIDS. There was only one picnic table, so the three of us squeezed in next to the old couple and ate our sandwiches.

Where are you headed? the man asked.

Um, Murdo? I said.

Never heard of it, he said.

I told him I hadn't either until yesterday.

Honey, said the woman, ask your mom for a napkin. She was talking to Thebes, who had mayonnaise and mustard running down her face.

Logan ignored us all. He had his giant air traffic controller headphones on and his hoodie up and was staring intensely at the chihuahua like he was wondering what the most painful way of killing it might be.

Is that your natural colour of hair? the man asked Thebes.

Yo! Dude! It's purple! What do *you* think?

I gave her a nudge under the table and passed her a paper bag to wipe the stuff off her face. She put it over her head and drew a face on it, blind. Big cartoon eyes and a mouth where the nose should be. I told her to go get the

Frisbee, and without removing the bag she stumbled and weaved and crashed her way to the van. She finally took the bag off her head and she and I threw the Frisbee around for a while before Logan joined in. He tried to make each of his throws deflect off the van's windshield and then he decided that we should play Frisbee *through* the van, with both side doors open and Thebes sitting on the seat *in* the van. She was entirely down with that and Logan had a blast whipping the Frisbee inches from her face, until he accidentally hit her and her nose bled, she cried, he apologized, said she was stand-up for playing the game, apologized again, and again, she forgave him with a karate kick to the 'nads, which he handled with an off-hand grace, said he deserved it, the old people shook their heads like bobblehead dolls and we all hit the road once again.

We kept driving south down the I-29, past the tiny hamlets of Wahpeton and Harkinson and Sisseton. Thebes said we should drive in directions that spelled something, like a giant word carved by us into the American landscape.

What word did you want to spell? I asked her.

Min, she said.

I traced the letters of my sister's name in my mind and realized there were no curves, so it might even have been possible to write her name in giant, hundred-mile-long letters if the roads had matched up with the lines, but they didn't. There were rivers and mountain ranges and deserts and gullies that separated *M-I-N* from posterity on the map.

By the time the sun had almost set, the kids had dozed off again. Thebes was curled up in a ball in the front now and Logan had stretched out in the back. I could hear the faint bass coming from his headphones and ice cubes sloshing around in the cooler. Giant, endless semis blasted past us and I waved to the drivers every time but they couldn't see me in the dark. I was looking for a cheap motel with a pool and free breakfast.

Thebes woke up and asked me what was going on. Help me find a motel, I said.

Will you give me a dollar?

Yeah.

What kind of motel?

Like in *Psycho*—have you seen it?

Yeah, she said.

Yeah? I said. Really? Aren't you kind of young?

Everybody knows *Psycho,* she said.

Yeah, but it's an old movie, I said.

Logan owns the original, said Thebes. She started doing the music from the shower scene. She told me that one time she'd pulled a Norman Bates on Min and it had gone badly. She was in the shower so I decided to attack her, she said. It wasn't a good idea. It was a bad choice, like they say in Guidance, she told me, which I never go to any more, by the way, since Mrs. Zefferelli told us that ultimately we're all alone in the world. Oh, said Thebes, going into one of her voices. Like, thanks, man! You're the Guidance teacher and you're basically, like, okay, kids, get lost, every man to himself, you're a rock, I'm an island, we're alone, we have no one, we die and then we rot. Scene.

What happened with the Norman Bates thing? I asked her.

Min screamed, she said. Okay, that worked. But then she stopped screaming and she sat down in the corner of the shower and started crying. I just stood there on the other side of the curtain and whispered that I was sorry and all that. I didn't know what to do. And then I decided to stick my hand around the curtain and try to hold Min's hand.

Did you find it? I asked.

Yeah, said Thebes, she took my hand and so we were just holding hands like that, with the curtain between us. And she was sitting down all naked and crying. My sleeve was getting soaked but I didn't mind.

That's nice, though, I said. I mean . . . holding her hand like that. Like walking in the rain.

And then I told her again that I was sorry for scaring her, said Thebes. I told her I was being Norman Bates, and she was all, like, she knew that, she just hadn't been expecting it, that's all.

Mmm, yeah, well . . . , I said.

And then, said Thebes, I realized my Norman Bates would never work if she expected to expect it every time. I mean the whole point—

Yeah, I said. Yeah.

Thebes spotted a motel, low-slung with lots of neon, a tiny outdoor pool and a basketball net. There was a permanent vacancy sign flickering on and off in the window next to the front desk and a sign that said No Repares Aloud in Lot. Logan shot hoops outside in the dark while Thebes and I checked in.

He's gonna have to stop that at eleven, said the woman behind the desk.

When we got to the room we stood next to the bed and stared at it. Thebes still had half-moons of dried blood around the edges of her nostrils from being hit in the face with the Frisbee. Do you ever wash? I asked her. Am I supposed to tell you to?

She decided that instead we'd all go swimming. She told me to go over to the window and look outside while she changed into her bathing suit.

There were two people sitting in a car in the parking lot, an older guy in a suit and a girl with a ponytail and an orange ball cap. The girl was giving the guy a hand job. Her arm was flying back and forth fast, like a school kid rubbing out mistakes with an eraser. It looked painful. The guy's eyes were squeezed shut.

Tada! said Thebes.

Hey, cute suit, I said. Let's go! I tried to hustle her away from the window.

You don't even have your bathing suit on, she said. I'll look away and you can change.

No, I don't feel like swimming, I said. I'll watch you, though. I could throw things into the water that you could dive for. Hey, I said, did you know that right after you were born Min and Cherkis put you in a little pool and you swam, naturally, like a champ.

Really? said Thebes. Were they trying to drown me?

No, I said, of course not, it was just something that they'd heard infants knew how to do.

———

Years ago I'd asked my mother the same question about Min. Had she been trying to drown me in Acapulco? She said well, no, she didn't think so, Min had been scared and frantic and hadn't known that she was pushing me under, that was all. After a while, I let the story stand. I hadn't wanted to believe my version of it anyway.

At our father's funeral Min held my hand and whispered in my ear that she'd take care of me, that she'd make sure I was okay, that she'd be strong for both of us. I nodded yeah, great, thanks, does that caring come with a complimentary drowning, because didn't you just try to . . . but no, I didn't say that. But I did pull my hand out of hers and stick it in the waistband of my ugly dress so she wouldn't try holding it again. I never doubted her conviction and her desire to be strong for both of us but I got this idea into my head that Min wanted me dead in order to protect me from some horrible danger in life that only she knew about, a fate *worse* than death, as they say. That she *was,* in fact, trying to take care of me. I wanted to ask her about that and have it all verified. But how do you begin a conversation like that? If she had come right out and said it, Hattie, I wish you were dead, I'd have nodded in acknowledgment. I'd have told her calmly that I knew it. And maybe, from that admission, we could have established a new way of being sisters. One that might have had me looking over my shoulder frequently but at least it would have been out in the open.

———

Logan and Thebes goofed around in the pool and I used our Frisbee to scoop a dead bird out of the shallow end when they weren't looking. Logan was floating on his back with an empty plastic wineglass balanced on his stomach and Thebes was trying to fill it up with filthy pool water that she was squirting through her teeth. Then the hand-job girl came cannonballing into the pool from out of nowhere, or the parking lot, and bobbed over to Logan and Thebes.

Are y'all saved? she asked.

From what, yo? said Thebes. Logan ignored the girl and kept floating around on his back, balancing the glass.

The wrath of Christ, said the girl.

Oh, that, said Thebes. I don't know if we all are saved. Let me put it to my bro. Logan? Are we all saved from the wrath of Christ?

I am the wrath of Christ, said Logan.

Oh, said Thebes. Hold up. I'll ask my aunt. Hattie! she said. Are we all saved from the—?

Thebes, I said, shhhhh. Yeah, we are. Tell her we are.

Word, said Thebes. Yeah, we check out, she told the girl. Wanna play Keep It Up?

So they played together awhile and I tried not to let the whole thing disturb the hell out of me.

Later on Logan and Thebes fought about what to watch on TV and who should hold the remote and decided somewhat mutually on *Nick at Nite* and that nobody would hold the remote. I went to the lobby to make just a phone call to France. I knew he'd be in India but I just wanted to hear his voice on the answering machine. I was wrong, though.

Marc said hello.

Hey! I said.

Hey, he said. Oh, hi!

Aren't you supposed to be in India?

Oh, yeah . . . well, yeah. Yeah.

Yeah.

Yeeeahhh . . .

Oh man.

Hey . . .

No, really, I said. Why am I such a loser?

You're not a loser, he said. Where are you?

I'm not sure.

Well . . . where are you?

I really don't know, I said. South Dakota.

Wow.

How's your centre?

What? he asked. What are you talking about?

Did you find it? I asked.

Hey . . . c'mon.

Hey . . . go fuck yourself.

You woke me up in the middle of the night to tell me . . .

I hung up and then phoned back. I'm sorry, I said.

No, no, he said. I had nothing to be sorry about. He was sorry. Really sorry. I started to cry. I listened to him tell me how beautiful and cool I was. Major kiss-off. It was so untrue. It was pathetic.

I really thought you were going to an ashram, I told him.

I really was going to, he said. Hey, can I put you on speaker?

No, don't, I said, okay? Just . . . And then what happened?

Well, he said, now he was kind of seeing someone.

Yeah, I said. I rested my head against the phone booth. The woman behind the front desk was staring at me.

Yeah, he said. So . . . yeah. Yeah. Yeahyeahyeahyeah.

I couldn't stop crying. I was trying to.

Hey, Hat, he said. We had a great time. We had a good run.

Yeah, I said. No bigger blast on earth.

We really did, he said.

Yeah. Neither one of us said anything for a while. Well, I said finally, I have to go back to the room.

What room? he said.

My motel room. I have to check on the kids.

What kids? he asked.

See you later, I whispered. *Namaste.*

Thebes wouldn't let me back in the room. She thought it was hilarious. Please, please open the door, I said. I started to cry all over again.

I saw her eye through the peephole. Then the door whipped open and she said, Holy Moly, I'm just kidding around, Hattie, what's wrong?

There's no mini-bar in here, is there? I said, and then

flung myself onto the bed and wept like Jesus and was sweetly consoled by my sister's children there in that shit-ass motel room in the middle of nowhere.

I told them how pathetic I'd been, calling France just to hear a recorded voice and then being dumped all over again. Thebes wiped my forehead with a cool washcloth, something she said Min did for her when she was feeling sick, at least she used to, and told me a joke. How much does a polar bear weigh?

I don't know, I said.

Enough to break the ice, hi, my name's Thebes, can I buy you a drink?

Logan said, That's not a joke, that's a lame pickup line. Then he said, Relationships, man . . . life is easy compared to relationships. Wanna smoke a joint?

Ater-lay, I told him.

Hey, said Thebes, I'm the one who invented Pig Latin. She pointed her finger at Logan. And don't forget, little man, you need *pot* to spell *impotent*. She stared hard at him and he told her to shut up, but he was laughing. I told Logan it was really stupid to bring pot, not to mention knives, across the border and he said he hadn't brought pot across the border, he'd got it from the girl in the pool. I didn't know when that had happened. Kids are sneaky.

Thebes sang "Happiness Is a Warm Gun." And then we all fell asleep together in the saggy stained bed while reruns of *Laverne and Shirley* and *The Odd Couple* droned on all night long and rats raided our cooler during breaks from relay-racing in the walls. I decided we'd look for partial rather than total dives from now on.

six

I WOKE UP BEFORE THE KIDS and noticed that Thebes had left a small silver notebook by the bed. Logan had covered himself up completely with his blanket. I couldn't see him but I could hear him snoring softly, humming, like a little airplane lost in the clouds. I picked up Thebes's notebook.

Road trip. First day. We are in America. I've been profiled at the border as a retard, by Logan. They still let me in. Hattie is sad about her boyfriend in Paris. He doesn't like her any more. Logan told her Internet dating was making a comeback and I told her to try to meet a whale, they mate for life. Ha ha. Logan hit me in the face with the Frisbee. The good thing is we're all saved. I miss you. I love you. I won't forget the important things.

I went to the lobby again and phoned the hospital and asked to speak to Min. The nurse said that wouldn't be possible right then . . . could they give her a message? Why isn't it possible? I asked.

Are you family? she said.

Yeah, I'm her sister, I said. The woman didn't think she had the authority to talk about Min's situation right then, but I could leave my number and she would get the doctor to call me back later in the day after rounds.

Well, I said, I'm not . . . I don't have a number. I'm at a pay phone.

Well, said the woman, will you be able to be reached later on in the day?

Well, I said, no. Is there a good time to call back? Then she told me that she believed the patient was having some difficulty speaking. That she was not quite ready to participate in normal daily routines. Yeah, I could understand that.

Hey, I said, my sister is alive, right? I immediately regretted it.

Yes, of course! said the woman.

I appreciated her emphatic confirmation, I did, but I asked her again if she was sure about that. Like, had somebody checked on Min in the last hour?

She's resting at the moment, said the woman. It'll take some time. She is alive, don't worry.

I thanked her and hung up and briefly considered turning right around and going back. I felt like the kid at the end of the five-metre diving board. I didn't really want to jump but there were twenty kids behind me lined up and yelling at me to go.

Thebes was loading the stuff into the van and Logan was picking and rolling around the parking lot with his basketball, periodically banging it off stuff like the van and the window at the front desk. The woman inside banged back and then came and told us to clear on outta there. There was a large black oil slick under the van.

Shotgun, said Thebes.

Already dibsed it, said Logan.

I hate you, said Thebes.

We were back on the road.

Thebes rooted around in the cooler and made us all peanut butter sandwiches for breakfast. Logan let her use his knife to cut them up but made her promise not to lick it. She wiped it on her filthy, rotting terry cloth shorts.

Did you bring other clothes? I asked her. How do you get so dirty anyway?

Just by way of my life, she said. What did Min say?

She said hi and sends big hugs and kisses, I said. Hopes we're having fun. Thebes smiled and moved her purple head from side to side like her favourite song had just come on the radio. Logan glanced at me, sideways, briefly, entirely hip to my bullshit. I honked the horn for no reason and whispered, Murdo, baby. Let's go.

It was my turn for a CD. I put in some Lucinda Williams and Logan said noooooooooooooooooooooo. He covered his face with his hands. Please, no, please, he said. I'm begging you.

C'mon, I said, it's not country. Check out the lyrics. I tossed the CD case into his lap. He screamed and tossed it back at me like it was a shitty diaper. Just put on your headphones then, I said. I'm playing it. I might play it on my next turn too. I've got a broken heart.

Logan took out his knife and started carving in the dashboard again. I wasn't going to try to stop him any more. I wanted to figure out what all his carvings meant. If the dashboard was his canvas, so be it. Who cares if it lowered resale value. It was a Ford Aerostar.

If I was a band I'd be breaking up, he wrote. The glove compartment door fell open and all the stuff inside fell out and he cursed and picked it up and rammed it back in and it wouldn't shut and for the next five or ten minutes he kept kicking it, over and over, trying to keep it closed.

Hey, said Thebes, from the back, how's morale up there? She asked Logan if he needed an oversized novelty cheque because she sure could make him one if he wanted, she had all the art supplies necessary. I peeked at her in the rear-view mirror. It looked like she'd cut her own hair along the sides. Logan took a roach out of his pocket and stuck it in his mouth.

Hey, no, you can't do that, smarten up, I said. Give me that. I tried to grab the thing out of his mouth but he moved his head and then grabbed my wrist in mid-air and held it there for an improbable amount of time. And I realized he wanted to be holding my wrist or at least holding something warm and human so we drove awhile like that, him holding up my arm like it was a big fish he'd caught and he was eight years old and having his picture taken.

We flew past animated families enjoying things like waterslides and go-karts and minigolf. My CD was over and it was quiet in the van. Nobody was talking and it was making me nervous for some reason. I couldn't stop thinking about Min, about what I should be doing, about how I had answered her question, her request, Help me die, and if it had been entirely wrong. The alternative seemed insane. Was I supposed to have agreed to kill my sister? Would that have bought her a little more time and made her happy? Just knowing that she had an out if she really, truly needed one? That her little sister would come along and knock her out with a hammer or something? Put a pillow over her face? What was I supposed to have said? Was it the least I could do considering that from the day I was born my sister had wanted to die?

None of us moved in our seats. We were all para- lyzed, lethargic and irritable. Like we were a bunch of recently beached whales who hadn't known each other in the sea and weren't about to hook up out of the sea, but there we were, together, incapable of moving and stuck with each other.

Then Thebes spoke. What does it mean when a person asks, Is that a gun in your pocket or are you just happy to see me?

Are you stupid? asked Logan.

Don't call her stupid, I said.

I didn't call her stupid, said Logan, I asked if she was. Then he paused and said skaaaaa in a voice that meant he thought she was a loser for playing the sax in a ska band at school.

What does that have to do with anything? she asked. Are you clueless or didn't you know that ska is all the rage in Mexico City?

So go there, said Logan. Want a ride to the airport?

Hey, said Thebes, what does "Do Not Siphon Gas by Mouth" mean? There was a sign at that gas station.

It means don't steal the gas with a siphon, with your mouth, I said.

What do you mean? she asked.

I don't know. I think just don't suck the gas from the nozzle, like with a tube or whatever, and then spit it into your own car? Maybe. I'm not sure. There was actually an official sign that said that? I asked.

Who would do that? said Thebes. Like, who would suck gas from a car?

I don't know, I said. People who really want gas.

Godspell, said Thebes. What's so great about gas?

Just say "god," Thebes, said Logan.

Hey, said Thebes, what does "Gonna Git Me Some" mean?

I don't know, I said.

Hattie, said Logan. He looked at me. Like, *Don't fall for this shit.*

I'm not sure, I said. It's like a really rude thing an idiot guy would say about, uh . . . being with a girl, or woman.

What do you mean? asked Thebes.

I don't know, I said.

You mean like "gonna git me a woman"? asked Thebes.

Yeah, but like . . . You know what? I said. It just . . . it's a sexual reference, okay? A total moron who wants to have sex with someone, probably someone as stupid as he is.

Thebes was quiet for a bit. Maybe twenty, thirty seconds.

"If This Is Tourist Season, Why Can't I Shoot 'Em?" she said. We'd seen that bumper sticker on a truck that had passed us earlier. What does that mean? she asked.

It's a joke, I said. Like hunting season? Tourist season?

Yeah, but why would you—

Fuuuuuck! said Logan. Shut the fuck up! He kicked the glove compartment door and the stuff poured out onto the floor again.

Logan, cut it out! I said.

Yeah, but she's intentionally being stupid and you're—

Logan, she's not intentionally being stupid!

Hey, said Thebes, unsure. Hey!

I think Thebes knew what all that stuff meant, it was true. She just wanted to know the three of us, her ad hoc family, were alive and that we still had enough juice to react to each other's bullshit. But I understood Logan's frustration. She likes to talk, I said to him. I shrugged. It's better than not talking, right? I said.

He stared out the window.

———

We drove through a town called Kennebec. We were getting close to Murdo. When we saw a beat-up looking basketball court next to an empty swimming pool, Logan asked if we could stop so he could shoot some hoops. He'd been holding his basketball in his lap like a sleeping newborn for hours. I pulled up next to the court and he turned around and chucked his ball at Thebes.

Yo, T., heads up, he said. She caught it, thrilled to death that he wanted to play with her, and they were off.

I lay down in the prickly brown grass next to the court and watched them play. Thebes would get the rebounds and pass them back to Logan or try to block him. Sometimes she'd sit beside me on the sidelines and yell like she was his coach.

The backboard exists for a reason, Troutman! she'd say. Wake up! She took off her shoe and threw it on the ground in despair. Stay with your man, Troutman! A couple of maintenance men in white overalls walked over to where we were sitting. They asked me what we were doing there and I said we were just resting, playing some basketball, hanging out.

Nobody ever comes here, said one of the men.

I said, Yeah, I can see that. I wondered what exactly these guys were maintaining. The kids came over and asked me what was up. We're just talking, I said. One of the guys asked Logan his name.

Logan said Lloyd Banks, and the guy took out a pen and wrote that down on the back of an envelope. Then he asked Thebes her name, and she said Veronica Lodge, and he wrote that down too. He asked them where they were from, the island of Togo? And then they laughed and said they were kidding. Logan said they were from Riverdale, Thebes's dream town. They wrote that down too.

Why are you writing this stuff down? I asked one of the guys.

He said they were doing an independent survey to determine who and what type of people use the playground.

After they left, we all sat on the grass and talked about who they might be. Aliens, religious freaks, FBI, scouts for the Lakers. Then Logan told Thebes that the best way to deal with school and life is to pretend that everyone is stoned. The teachers, mom, friends, me, the bus driver, grandma when she was alive, kids, everyone. So that when someone says to you something like, Thebes, we're worried about your home life, or Thebes, it's come to our attention that you've missed sixteen consecutive band practices, or Hey, kid, you've gotta pay to ride the bus, you can just laugh and laugh at the lunacy of it all. Then Thebes went over to the van and took out a giant novelty cheque she'd made for Logan. It was about four feet long. She'd made it with cardboard and markers and Popsicle sticks for ballast on the back so it wouldn't bend. She brought it over to us and looked at Logan, who squinted up at her, one hand blocking the sun that made her look like she was on fire.

I'd like to present this to you, Logan, for . . . I'm not sure what, she said.

She just likes making oversized novelty cheques, he explained to me. I get them all the time. How much is it worth? he asked her.

One million dollars, she said. Congratulations for being my brother. She held it in front of his face and he took it and looked at it.

Thanks, Thebes, he said.

Do you make a speech now? I asked him.

No, he said.

Don't worry, you'll get one too, said Thebes. She sat down on the grass again and then lay down and put her head in my lap. While she braided grass, I pulled some art supply stuff out of her hair and blew in her face. There's no way you'll be able to comb your hair, I told her. You'll have to shave your head or grow dreads.

I know, she said.

I gently massaged her scalp. It was discoloured from the purple dye and speckled with dirt and glue and glitter. Hey, I said, where's the scalpel stuck?

Here, she said, and guided one of my fingers over to the right side of her head.

Does it ever hurt? I asked her.

Nah, she said.

We were quiet, watching dragonflies and braiding grass.

This is way better than being in Paris with that Gandhi guy, right? she said.

Logan stared off at the highway. I admired his tactful restraint. I liked the way he didn't *always* correct her, how he sometimes just turned away and let things go.

———

Driving the home stretch into Murdo. It was a tiny, innocu-
ous speck of a thing on the map, but for us, at least for me,
it loomed large suddenly like the shadow of King Kong, or
like we were approaching the Kandahar city limits in the
back of a U.S. tank with a giant American flag. It scared
me. I had no plan, really. Well, I had a plan. I had an outcome planned. But I had no real plan that would logically
get me to the plan's outcome, which was, of course, to find
Cherkis and beg him to take care of his kids. I didn't want
to. I didn't know how to. I didn't know what to say to them
or how to comfort them. I wondered if Min believed in a
random world or one with a divine purpose. There were so
many things we hadn't talked about and now it all seemed
too late. Sometimes she could pull the parenting thing off
on her own, get things done, function, we'd laugh on the
phone, I'd visit maybe once a year, it was fun, normal, but
then . . . who knows what happened. Water through her
fingers. Sand, air. It slipped away.

When I was eight years old I spent an entire week living
among three wards of the biggest hospital in town. My
father was having his gallbladder removed, my mother was
having a balloon inserted somewhere into her body and
Min was locked up in the psych ward. I would spend twenty
minutes, silently, at each bedside, and then spend twenty
minutes searching every vending machine for change.
Then I'd spend twenty minutes reading trashy magazines in

whichever waiting area I felt like sitting in, and then I'd start all over again. It was really important to me that every thing I did in the hospital lasted no more and no less than twenty minutes. It was my twenty-minute survival plan. You can do anything for twenty minutes. You can survive. Maybe not underwater, but otherwise.

Did you know, said Thebes, that most but not all secret agents have blue eyes?

No, I said.

There was a pen museum in Murdo, apparently. I saw one of those beat-up signs on wheels by the side of the road. Someone had changed the museum's "slogan" to The Penis Mightier Than the S Word. I willed Thebes not to comment on it but she was busy constructing something less mighty in the back seat anyway and didn't notice. Someone who has a *pen museum* in a place like Murdo could very well have known Cherkis, who after all had a *crap museum* in Murdo, and how many whacked-out DIY curators can live in a town this size without knowing each other?

I followed the directions to a storefront on Main Street. Logan and Thebes were suddenly very alert, like we were poised to launch a sting op and bring it all down.

Right there, said Logan. He pointed at the building.

Thebes jumped out of the van before I could put it in park. She was carrying another one of her homemade novelty cheques, written out to Cherkis for a thousand dollars. Logan got a million, I thought. How does she decide, or does she just run out of space for zeros and then quit?

Thebes, I said, I don't think he's here any more. I'm just gonna talk to whoever *is* here and find out if they know where he *might* be.

Cool, baby, cool, said Thebes. The wind was howling and she was struggling to keep herself and the giant cheque from flying away. Logan had his security blanket ball with him and threw it once against the side of the van and said, Coming? We went into the pen museum together.

A middle-aged woman sat like Christ in the Last Supper at a long wooden table covered with stuff, mostly pens, yeah, and we all said hi.

Are you here to see the pens? she asked.

Um, well, yeah, I said. But I also—

So, that'll be, um . . . she was doing some mental math that for the final sum seemed a tad laborious . . . three dollars altogether. One each. What is that? she asked Thebes.

A cheque, said Thebes.

I gave the woman three bucks and the kids and I scanned the pens for about a minute until I could muster up the guts to pop the question. So, uh, excuse me, I said to the woman, these are righteous pens but would you happen to know or to have known a guy named Cherkis who lived around here years ago and also had a small museum/gallery thing? Outside of town maybe? Like, in a field? In an old house?

Yeah, of course I knew Cherkis, she said. Are you his wife?

I said no.

Girlfriend?

No, no.

Ex-girlfriend? she asked.

No, just an old friend from high school, I said, like back in Canada. We're travelling around, me and, uh, these guys, and I remembered that he used to live here and I thought maybe he still did and I'd pop in on him and say hello. Thebes sucked in some air, loudly. I thought about putting her in a headlock and clamping my hand over her mouth.

Yo, Thebie, said Logan, c'mere. He'd wandered over to the other side of the room to check out the quill section. She hopped over to him and he whispered something in her ear.

So we found out from the woman that Cherkis had burned his house down and left for maybe California. Well, *he* hadn't burned his house down, she said, some kids or whatnot might have, or maybe a cigarette, or lightning, or a bushfire that got out of control. It could have been from cooking, or faulty wiring or possibly a random act of God. She had about five thousand other potential inferno scenarios. I didn't really care how his house burned, I just wanted to know where he was in California. If she knew. She said she thought he had some artist friends, some Burning Man types, in the desert outside of L.A. somewhere. Then she said she'd quickly call up Rosie at the Something-something and ask her if she knew where he'd gone. Rosie had done yoga with Cherkis a few times and had fed his dogs when he was away. The woman said Rosie and Cherkis had tried to start some film thing, like showing old movies once a week on a big outdoor screen.

The kids and I waited. Please don't touch the pens, she told Thebes, who was drawing on herself with a pen shaped like either a rocket or a dildo.

The woman made the call and said, Uh-huh, uh-huh, uh-huh, uh-huh, uh-huh, okay, uh-huh, uh-huh, okay, no, she passed away in her sleep, okay, yeah, her sleep, okay, thanks, Rosie. She hung up.

Twentynine Palms, she said. Near that park, Joshua Tree? That's about all she knows.

Does she know what he's doing there? I asked the woman. Do they correspond?

Nope, said the woman. That's all ancient history. Probably still collecting, she said, doing his art. Whatnot.

Do you know when he left? I said.

Probably three, four years ago, she said. You gonna drive all the way to California just to say hi to an old friend from high school?

Yeah, maybe, I said. Why not? I smiled. The kids were already heading for the door. I thanked her and told her she had a superlative and somewhat awesome pen collection.

She said, You know it, honey, best in the west.

But you should check out your mobile sign thing on the highway, I said. Somebody messed with it.

Jesus, this town, she said. She continued to speak disparagingly of her community and all the assholes in it. I mean, she said, what kind of monster . . . Who would do something like that?

Yeah, yeah, I know, I said. I would have stood around talking about the rather huge gap between bored kids pranking around and hate crimes, but Thebes was blasting the horn and we had a desert ahead of us.

So, said Logan.

So, I said.

Sounds like Cherkis is a bit of a . . . Logan didn't finish.

A what? I said.

Yoga? he said.

Hey, yoga's a good thing, I said. What's wrong with yoga?

Logan opted not to explain. His current hero was the guy who cut off his arm with a pocket knife after being pinned under a rock for a few days and then walked five miles or something covered in blood holding onto his stub.

Maybe half an hour went by and I decided to answer my own question. There's nothing wrong with yoga, Logan, I said.

Whatever, said Logan.

Are you trying to come up with reasons not to find him? I said. Do you want to go back?

No, said Logan, I'm just saying.

Yeah, I said, but what are you saying?

Nothing, said Logan.

Yoga is a meditative thing, I said. So he's looking for a little peace of mind.

I'm not talking about yoga, said Logan.

Then what are you talking about? I asked.

Nothing!

Cherkis is . . . I didn't know what to say. He's . . . he used to carry you around on his shoulders all the time, I said. Min was always scared he'd drop you.

Did he? asked Logan.

No, never, I said.

It started to rain. I turned on the wipers and the one on the driver's side flew off and disappeared into the ether.

Great, I said. Fantastic. I pulled over to the shoulder and got out of the van to check it out. I didn't know what I was checking out. I climbed back in the van and turned on the wipers again. The skinny metal thing was still screeching back and forth but the black rubber part that goes over it was gone.

Let's wrap a T-shirt or something around it, said Thebes.

Okay, give me one, I said. She handed me one of Logan's. It said *Dick's Pizza Call 474-DICK* on it.

Not one of mine, said Logan. Use yours. Thebes said she hadn't packed any other clothes. She'd forgotten about clothes.

This kid's a disaster, said Logan, and he cranked the volume on his CD. I looked at the case. He'd drawn some strange things on it, skeletal creatures, and written up a play list.

Mudhoney—March to Fuzz
Bad Religion—All Ages
The Germs—(MIA): The Complete Anthology

Crucifucks—Our Will Be Done
The Natural History—The Natural History (EP)
Dead Kennedys—Fresh Fruit for Rotting Vegetables
Talib Kweli and Hi-Tek—Reflection Eternal
Public Enemy—It Takes a Nation of Millions to Hold
    Us Back
OutKast—Aquemini
Sparta—Wiretap Scars

I got some duct tape from Thebes's art box and taped Logan's T-shirt to the metal wiper rod. I was wet and cold and tired and pissed off. I got back in the van and tested the wiper. The shirt unravelled from the rod and fell onto the hood of the car.

Hey, said Logan, I know how you can get rid of that arm flab with different weightlifting techniques.

Thebes asked me what a Passion play was.

We sat by the side of the road in the rain listening to Logan's CD. Not a lot of traffic passed us. I fell asleep for five minutes and dreamt that I was pregnant with Marc's baby and we were deliriously happy and proud. When I woke up it had stopped raining and the Crucifucks were silent and Thebes and Logan were gone. Two seconds later they popped up from the ditch by the side of the road and got back in the van and handed me some wet red and yellow flowers that Thebes then insisted on weaving into my hair while I drove and Logan said it was okay if I wanted to take two CD turns and play Lucinda Williams or any of that other shit I had with me.

Logan was leafing through his notebook. He read me

his personal ad, an odd assignment he had to do for
Family Studies:

> I am fifteen years old. I am a consistent B student
> and enjoy watching football and other things on
> television. I like gambling and am extremely
> wealthy. I enjoy films and music of all kinds. I like
> many different kinds of food and desserts includ-
> ing breakfast. I hate the cold and own many warm
> garments. I like people who are easygoing and
> have a crazy sense of humour. No member of my
> family is "known" by the police and I am relatively
> well-adjusted.

That's a lie, I said. You're known by the police.
Not really, he said.
What about when you kidnapped that guy?
We didn't *kidnap* a guy. He was our friend and we
just threw him into the trunk for a while and drove
around.
Min had called me in Paris in the middle of the night
to tell me that Logan had been taken into custody and was
being questioned by the cops. They questioned each of
his friends separately and the story that came out was that,
okay, yeah, chill, man, he and his buddies had planned this
kidnapping for the hell of it, basically. They'd grabbed one
of their friends off the street, from behind, wearing bala-
clavas, shoved a blanket over his head, thrown him into
the trunk of one of their dads' cars and then driven
around town drinking Red Bull and Jag. The kid had been

scared shitless at first but had laughed it off in the end. His parents, though, didn't see it as such a kick and went to the cops.

What eventually happened? I asked Logan.

Nothing, he said.

That's the case so often, isn't it, I said.

Not really, said Logan. Often things do eventually happen.

Well, there's that, I said. You guys still friends?

Of course! said Logan. What do you think?

I loved that. I loved that Logan and his friends could plot secretly to kidnap another friend of theirs, scare the hell out of him, probably almost suffocate him, definitely scrape him up a bit by throwing him around and everything, get his parents on their asses, not to mention the law, and still come out, *natch,* as friends! Beautiful.

Logan was quizzing Thebes with a German accent. He'd spent about five minutes getting his hair to stand straight up. Now he was asking her scientific questions about histograms and grids and bio-amplification.

Thebes told us about her book report. She'd taken one of Min's books: *Clara Callan.* I wrote that Clara is independent, said Thebes, and makes her own decisions. She decides that she doesn't believe in God and that she will stop going to church. Another decision she makes is to have an abortion in New York City after being raped by a monkey-faced hobo near the train tracks. I concluded that I thought these were excellent decisions because it means Clara is taking control of her own life, and because I knew Min would like the sound of that.

Logan told us there were three girls with babies in his Family Studies class.

Really? I said. And the fathers?

He shook his head slowly, sighed like a burned-out social worker with an impossible caseload, and said in a fake earnest voice, Yup, where are the fathers?

seven

I WONDERED WHAT WAS HAPPENING TO MIN right now. Was she strapped to a gurney with wires stuck to her head and a spoon in her mouth, wild eyes, and eighteen thousand sparky volts of electroshock frying her brain, filling up the spaces with smoke and ash, and helping her to reconfigure her negative thinking into something less painful but empty? I imagined her doctor sitting in a room next to hers, staring at a computer screen, saying boo-yeah! with every direct hit to her memory target. Or who knows, maybe she was strong enough to sit up and join the "Koombaya" gang in the common room. *Hey there, Min, what do you see down by the river?* Maybe she was enjoying a moment in her life, a sliver of light, a flash memory of one of her kids, something sweet and approaching reality.

I remembered Min telling me that Logan had had an imaginary friend for a while when he was three or four. His name was Jackson Whinny. He was a football star but he could never play because he was always injured and he only ate fast food and he lived with his mom even though he was a grown man because he needed her to take care of him and his injuries. His other imaginary friend was named Willie the Ghost, but he wasn't around too often. Min said Logan's little mind was creating a more gradual exit for the people who had once been in it and then— *BOOM*—one day weren't. She said he was subconsciously buying himself time to get his brain around it.

Hey, said Thebes, there's someone behind us flashing his lights. We're gonna get jacked!

I checked the rear-view mirror. Two guys in a half-ton. Logan turned around for a look.

Don't pull over, he said. Speed up.

No, that's dumb, I said. But I sped up anyway. Isn't this supposed to happen in Miami or something? I said.

We're all gonna die! said Thebes.

The truck drove along next to us and the guy in the passenger seat rolled his window down.

Just so you guys know, said Thebes, I love you with all my heart and even if you two don't have heaven-cred, I do, and I will put in a word with the Big Guy and tell—

Thebes, I said, will you please shut up.

I'll meet you on the other side, my friends! she said.

Here we go, said Logan. He pulled his hoodie way down over his face.

Circle of life, said Thebes. She threw her arms into the air.

That's not even original, said Logan. That's Bart Simpson—

You don't have to be original when your time is up, said Thebes. Word to yer mama.

Hey, what's up, I said to the guy. He was smiling. I smiled back.

Nice flowers, he said, pointing to my head.

Thanks, I said. We smiled some more. We could get this massacre over civilly at least.

You're dragging something, he said. Just wanted to let you know.

They took off, flashed their taillights goodbye, and I pulled over to the shoulder once again. Logan jumped out.

Fuck! He said. Fuck! We'd been dragging his head-phones for miles. The wire had been stuck in the door. They were all dusty and torn up. He went over to them and knelt down and picked them up and held them, swearing softly, bereft and tender, but mad as hell. Then he raised his face to the heavens, to his malevolent maker, and screamed, how could he live without his headphones! Why had this happened to him? What had he ever done?

Thebes popped her head out of the van and said that if he wanted to have a funeral for them in the field, she could lead it, no charge, "Amazing Grace," the works. I yanked her back inside and told her to leave him alone. She took a picture of him, boy grieving, with her disposable underwater camera. She and I gave him some time alone with his headphones.

I see Troutman corpses piling up, she said. We have to stop in the next town and get him new ones. Key to our survival.

Hey, she said. If Logan gets to get new headphones, could I get a crimping iron?

I don't know, I said. Maybe.

A crimping iron is twenty-five bucks, she said, but if you just think about it for a minute you'll soon realize that it'll be worth every last penny.

Let me think about it for one hour, I said. I'll need you not to talk to me during that time.

I want to make it to Cheyenne, Wyoming, I told the kids when we were back on the road.

It was smoking hot in the van and Logan took off his shirt and hoodie and climbed into the back and plunged his head into the cooler and then shook it. Water sprayed everywhere and Thebes screamed. Then she noticed a scar on his back.

Where'd you get that? she asked. She moved her finger lightly over his skin. He stared out the window.

Hey, she said, are you in a fight club?

You mean like the movie? he said.

Yeah, whatever, she said.

You mean like that movie *Fight Club*? he said.

Yeah, or you know, a variation on the theme, she said.

A variation on the theme of the movie *Fight Club*? he said.

Yeah! Like some local chapter, she said. You know? Starring Brad Pitt? Are you?

Am I a member of a local chapter that is a variation on the theme of the movie *Fight Club* starring Brad Pitt? he said.

I suggested to Thebes that she stop talking to Logan too, and write a story. Logan commended me on my first really excellent idea on the trip so far. Thebes didn't know what to write about. Logan told her to write about a guy in a small village in South America or something like that, who is driven away because everyone thought that he had died and they were seeing his ghost and so now he lives down the road and is trying to prove that he's alive so that he can go back and live in his village, which is all he wants out of life.

So, said Logan, the problem is, how does he prove he's alive?

Thebes said she would rather rewrite the Ten Commandments on a piece of dark blue construction paper with her special gold glitter pen.

Then fucking do it already! I said. I immediately apologized.

It's okay, said Thebes. Those are just words. Language isn't real.

Yes it is, said Logan.

Not to me, said Thebes.

How can it not be real to you? I said. You use it every day.

Yeah, I know, said Thebes, but that's all.

Okay, I said.

Like you know when it snows in May? said Thebes. How much that sucks?

Yeah, I said.

I don't let my brain accept the word *snow*, said Thebes.

Hmm, I said. Okay, so . . .

I pretend it's something else, she said.

The snow? said Logan.

Yeah, she said.

Like what? he said.

I don't know, said Thebes. Like stuff somebody left behind.

Hey, said Logan, you forgot your stuff. It's everywhere.

Yeah, I said, my dog's shitting all over your stuff.

See, said Thebes, exactly. Hey, how's this one?

What one? I said.

Be at Peace with Yourself in this Chaotic World, she said.

Is that one of your commandments? I asked. She said yeah.

Logan said it was too vague.

How about this, said Thebes. Do Not Let Hard Words Control Your Life.

I said yeah, that was a good one.

Logan said, What do you mean? Like *harsh* words? Or like *difficult, complicated* words.

Hard words, she said.

I think it should be clearer, said Logan. Write *harsh* or something. Or how about Do Not Let Hard Liquor Control Your Life.

Logan, just let Thebes make her own commandments, okay?

Fine.

Fine.

What about Be Kind to Dogs? asked Thebes.

What if a dog is attacking your best friend? said Logan. He was carving into the dash again.

Thebes, I said, just write your commandments down, every one you can think of.

She was quiet and then she started to say something. No, no, I said. Don't. Don't talk. I'm still thinking about that thing, that crimping iron, and you have to concentrate on your commandments. Let's all be quiet. Let's have a quiet contest.

Okay, she said, but just so you know? Glenn Gould could do his playing, his live performances, while reminding himself of people he had to call, the number of the cab he'd have to call later to get home, all that stuff, and none of it interfered with his playing.

Okay, I said. Boffo. I'm buying a tranquilizer gun in Cheyenne.

Hey, I whispered to Logan, how *did* you get that scar on your back? What happened?

Shhh, he said, quiet contest, remember?

Yeah, but, just—

Shhh . . .

This time Logan had carved the question *Who needs actions when you've got words? K. Cobain.* He had already changed the title of Thebes's secondary reading material to *Harry Pothead and the Philosopher's Stone.* Then he changed it to *Happy Pothead . . .* and then he changed it to *Happy Pothead and Phil Is Stoned.* I told him he'd have to buy Thebes a new book, but she doesn't want a new one. She wants the old one with the messed-up cover and the equivalent worth in Archie comics. Logan is reading *Twelve,* a book about drugs and parties and death in Manhattan, and *Heavier Than Heaven,* the Kurt Cobain biography, which is all about pretty much the same stuff and where he must have gotten the quote he'd just carved into the dash. He's got *The Tin Drum* and a George Saunders book and *Maus* and *Howl* and a book about *Saturday Night Live* all stuffed, along with his notebooks and sketchbooks, into a fake alligator-skin suitcase he bought at a Goodwill store for four dollars.

We drove through the heat. We didn't talk for a long time. Who needs words when you're having a quiet contest? I saw a fat guy walking slowly down the highway, hunched against the hot wind, with a faded marathon number pinned to his back. He looked tired. He was headed in the same direction as us. I wanted to talk to another adult.

I pulled up next to him and Logan rolled his window down and I leaned over and said hey.

Hey, said the guy. He barely looked at us.

We're going to Cheyenne, I said. Are you in a race?

He said no, he had been, but not any more.

Oh, I said, are you lost?

No, he said, not exactly. I liked this guy. We could become best friends, I thought. I live in a town eighty miles from here, he said. I'm the caretaker of a church.

Do you want to ride with us for a while? I asked him.

Thebes and Logan looked at me, looked at him, looked at me.

No thank you, he said.

You're gonna walk for eighty miles to get home? I asked him. He said he'd stop along the way. Where are you gonna stop? I asked him. He hadn't decided yet.

I was desperate to talk to this guy. He kept trudging down the highway and our van crept along beside him. I don't see any houses or anything around here at all, I said. He shrugged, nodded, yeah, no. So where are you going to stop? I asked him.

Points yonder, he said, and smiled.

Points yonder? I repeated. Nice. I smiled back. We kept our glacial pace and eased on down the road. C'mon, I said, hop in, just for a break. Aren't you tired? I said. He said he was but still, no thank you.

Is it because we're strangers? I asked him. He looked at us. He said he just wanted to walk if that was okay with me. Yeah, of course, I said, but how'd you get separated from the pack?

What pack? he said.

Your race! I said. I pointed at the number pinned to his back. Logan took a big breath and closed his eyes. The guy didn't say anything, just shook his head. Are you sure you don't want a ride, just for a few miles? I said. We won't hurt you, I promise.

He smiled wearily and said yeah, he was sure.

Do you want a drink or something? A bottle of water? Or we've got juice! Thebes! I said.

Yo! she said, and whipped the lid off the cooler and grabbed a bottle of water. Here, she said. She handed the water to Logan, who handed the water to the guy, who took it and said thank you very much.

Well, do you race often? I asked him.

He said no, it had been a stupid idea. He hadn't known what he was doing or what he was getting into. I loved this guy!

Listen, I said, why don't you just . . . get in the van.

Nope, he said. He told us he'd be just fine, really, but thank you.

I said yeah, I know but—

Jesus, Hat, whispered Logan, give it up, man, fuck.

I thought: Kidnap this odd walking man, be lost and tired together, take care of the church, laugh at our old misguided ways (Oh yeah, what were we thinking? Marathons. Searching for fathers. Hilarious!), change my name from Troutman to something like Grey . . .

Mmm-hmm, I said, cool. Okay. I smiled at the guy. Good luck with, you know, the whole . . . this, I told him, and took off.

Shh, I said to the kids, who were poised to explode with commentary. At least Thebes was.

Were you gonna marry that guy or what? she said.

Logan had said earlier what he'd needed to say. Filled his daily talking quota.

Hey, do you want to play Zit? said Thebes.

Not now, I said, okay, Thebie? I reached around and patted her stomach, although I'd been aiming for her knee. Your shirt is crusty, I told her. We'll have to cut it off you. Logan took out his knife. No, put that away, I said.

We were in Cheyenne, at a giant rodeo and carnival. The Granddaddy of 'em All, was what the sign said. We were floating over barns and corrals and concession stands and chuckwagons in a huge Ferris wheel. The kids were throwing mini-doughnuts at the crowds on the ground, because, according to Logan, it's tradition and it doesn't hurt. He had new headphones, but Thebes had decided to buy a plastic holster and two pistols instead of a crimping iron. She said she'd never take the holster off. Now both the kids were armed. When we were buying them a woman at the store had looked at Thebes and then at me and had said I should comb that girl's hair . . . was it purple? And what kind of a mother was I?

Um, inferior? I said.

We witnessed a robbery while we were in the store. A young guy, about twenty, came running in and grabbed as many bags of Huggies diapers as he could carry. He went tearing past us and one of them fell, and Logan picked it up and shovel-passed it to the guy, who said thanks, man, and kept on running.

Next time that guy wants to shoplift he should consider a pack of these bad boys, said Thebes, pointing one of her pistols at a row of Trojan condoms. She fired at them, and blew off the barrel like a pro. Am I right or am I right? she said.

We got off the Ferris wheel and wandered around. We bought some corn on the cob. We observed Americans at play. Logan was looking at girls. Staring at girls. Thebes took my hand and tried to take one of Logan's.

Don't, he said, and shook it off. We were liabilities, me and Thebes. She started to hum "To Sir with Love." Other kids were staring at her hair and her holster and her general prodigious strangeness. The fake tattoos she'd had all over her arms and legs had smeared and faded in the pool the other night and her skin had a rainbow glow to it that was pretty and unique in a way, but could also easily be mistaken for some awful skin disease.

Thebes wanted to watch some bullfighting.

It's not bullfighting, said Logan.

It's like bull . . . bull riding? I said.

Like, busting, he said, or whatever. Bronco busting. I don't know. It's not bullfighting. Okay, so Thebes wanted to watch the bulls and Logan said he was going to walk around for a while and check out some other stuff. We arranged to meet back by the Ferris wheel at ten, and then we'd go find a motel for the night.

Thebes and I watched cowboys get thrown off raging bulls and be rescued by clowns. She had pink cotton candy all over her face and arms and hands and legs and feet and shoulders and back. I wondered if she maybe didn't have scabies too. A nice old man sitting next to her let her borrow his watch so she could count off the eight seconds, the length of time the cowboys were supposed to stay on the bull's back. She yelled out the numbers in German and then French and then Spanish. She was very excited and had to be reminded constantly, by the family of haters behind us, to sit down and stay down, they'd paid their money to see the bronco bustin' and dang if they were gonna have some wild foreign retard leapin' up every second and blockin' their view.

Got that? I said to Thebes. I put my arm around her shoulders and pulled her in close to me. She gave the man his watch.

Thank you very much, she whispered. I'm sorry if it's sticky.

No problem, gunslinger, he said.

She watched the rest of the cowboys silently. Tears were running down her face and getting mixed up with the cotton candy.

Let's go, I said. I grabbed her hand and pulled her out of the bleachers and down the ramp and outside into the not-so-fresh night air. Lights were flashing and people were laughing and screaming. We walked over to a dark, empty piece of grass behind a heifer barn and sat down.

Go ahead, I said.

It's just that . . . , she said.

I know, I said.

It's just that . . . I'm not retarded, she said.

I know that, I said.

I just want Min, she said. She never yells at me. She thinks I'm beauti—

You are, I said. She couldn't get very far past that before it all erupted and she was sobbing in my arms and then all the captive little heifers in the barn next to us joined in, crying and lowing like a bovine choir of angels in solidarity with Thebes.

It was time to meet up with Logan at the Ferris wheel. Here, let me fix that, I said. I adjusted Thebes's holster so it hung slightly lower on her narrow hips. It was ten after ten and Logan wasn't at the Ferris wheel. Thebes and I shared another bag of mini-doughnuts and played Twenty Questions while we waited. After that she told me about her Tag manifesto. She'd written up a set of rules for Tag during recess at school.

1. *No time outs*
2. *No quitting and rejoining*
3. *No sore rebounding*
4. *No cliffhangers*
5. *No physical fighting or hurtful tagging*
6. *No stabbing*
7. *No pulling hats down*

Do people adhere to your manifesto? I asked her.

Yes, she said. Most of the time.

What happens if they break a rule? I asked.

Well, nothing, said Thebes. Because they're just *my* rules.

Stay right here and don't move, okay? I told Thebes. I'm just gonna take a walk around and see if I can find him. If he shows up here, make sure you guys both stay here. Don't leave. Okay?

Roger that, daddio, said Thebes. She had us do one of her elaborate hand shake-punch-slap-grab routines and I headed off in the direction of the arcade emporium. Logan wasn't there. He wasn't at the gambling booths either, or at the rodeo, or by any of the food stands or waiting in line for any of the rides. He wasn't watching the Miss Cheyenne pageant or the Cutest Little Buckaroo contest, and when I returned, he wasn't back waiting with Thebes, either.

Hmmmm, I said. What time is it, anyway? I asked Thebes. She'd been talking to the Ferris wheel operator about prime numbers.

Eleven twelve, she said. Shit. Hey, I said to the operator, you'll be here for a while, right? It's okay if she hangs out a little bit longer?

Totally, said the guy. I'm bored anyway.

I told Thebes I'd be back really soon, again, and that if Logan showed up, to stay there with him. I really didn't want to do all the high-five stuff with her again.

I went to the parking lot and found him in the van with a girl. They were making out on one of the back seats and didn't see me. I moved a few yards away and gently threw some bits of gravel at the side window. Logan popped his head up and then disappeared again. I waited for them to figure out what they'd do next. I looked at the sky, at the moon, at the position of the moon in the sky, at the formation of clouds surrounding the moon, back at the ground and up again.

Hey, I said, as they crawled out of the van.

Logan didn't say anything, but the girl said hi, um, hi, sorry.

No, no, I said. I shrugged. We smiled.

They were both wearing black hoodies. Logan kind of pawed at the girl's sleeve and gently pulled her over to a dark corner of the parking lot and said something to her and she had her hands in his front pockets and then he gave her a kiss and she walked away and he turned around and looked at me and then at the girl walking away and then for a second back at me, and then back at the girl again. I leaned against the van and lit a cigarette and told him Thebes was waiting all by herself with a guy at the Ferris wheel. He slowly walked over to me and I asked him if he wanted a cigarette.

I don't smoke, he said.

I was kidding, I said.

Can we not talk? he said.

Yep, deal, I said. Do you want to stay here while I go get Thebes?

He said yeah.

I noticed that he had silver and gold glitter on his face and in his hair. Were you guys doing crafts in there? I asked.

He looked away, towards Saturn, or farther up, maybe towards some satellite that only he could see. I liked the silver and gold specks. They softened him up. He looked like a sweet, kind of gay, raver alien waiting for his crew to take him back to space, to some benevolent planet that partied hard but happily. I left him to pine and sparkle in the moonlight.

Thebes and the Ferris wheel operator were sitting cross-legged on the grass, talking. When she saw me coming she jumped up and said, What? No Logan? What fresh hell is this? She told me that was Dorothy Parker, yo, props to her.

Yeah, I know, I said. It was Min's favourite combination of words. She said it all the time. I imagined she was still saying it.

I found him, I said, let's go, he's in the van.

What was he doing in the van? said Thebes.

Making out with a girl, I said.

We found a cheap motel and unloaded our paltry crap into the room. There was no pool, no free breakfast and no phones. Well, what do you have? I asked.

Beds, said the guy.

Who would just sit there and let someone suck on your throat for four hours or whatever it takes to create an entire hickey necklace? Thebes asked Logan. He was ignoring her, watching TV, and she was sitting next to his head and peering at his neck. That's the most disgusting thing I've ever seen in my life, said Thebes. Would you have let Gandhi do that to your neck, Hattie? she asked.

I shook my head and held my finger to my lips. I was studying the map on the other bed, trying to figure out how to get to Twentynine Palms.

You're lucky she didn't give you an aneurism, said Thebes. She could have sucked your jugular vein right out of you through your skin and you would have bled to death all over my art supplies.

Logan turned the volume up on the TV.

Thebes, I said, just leave him alone, okay? Why don't you see if you can find me some beer in the lobby or something. Or go get some ice. Get both.

Like, technically, said Thebes, that could be considered an assault. Look at these bruises! She moved her fingers gently over Logan's throat. You were attacked by a girl. Are you traumatized? She started humming "No Woman No Cry." She stopped humming. You were violated in there, she said, and now you're all calm watching TV and—

Logan whipped the pillow out from under his head and hit Thebes hard in the face. She screamed and fell off the bed. Logan got up and left the room and Thebes ran to the door and put the chain on and then went into the bathroom and locked that door too, until I finally talked her out and calmed her down and tried to explain some stuff about Logan to her.

She asked me if I thought he was depressed. I said no. He needs to know he's loved and safe and that he'll be able to eat when he's hungry and shoot hoops when he has to bust out and be attractive to girls and have friends to hang out with sometimes. Other than that, I said, there's not much to do but wait it out. He's fifteen. I compared Logan to a guy coming home to his apartment (our van/hotel room) to roommates he's ambivalent about (us) and just wanting to chill out and not be quizzed about anything. I said if he could replace us with a giant-screen TV right now he probably would.

Do you think he thinks a lot about Cherkis? she asked.

He might, I said. He might a lot, or maybe hardly at all. We can't really know. Maybe in five years he'll talk about it all to a girlfriend or his buddies or a therapist or a stranger in a bar, who knows. Maybe he'll blame Min, maybe Cherkis, maybe himself, maybe me. Maybe nobody. Maybe everybody. Maybe it'll be this thing he carries like a fucking cross all through his life, his eternal destiny, or maybe it won't really be a big deal at all.

You should have a talk with him, said Thebes.

I don't know what to say, I said.

Well, she said, you could just start out with talking about how you felt when you were fifteen.

There was a soft knock. Thebes catapulted over to the door and flung it open and threw her arms around her brother. He stood there for a minute and let her hug him, and then he patted her back a couple of times and looked at me for help. He still had a few sparkles on his face, under his eye and on his nose. For one second he looked just like Min when she was younger. Maybe it was the glitter. Maybe it was that expression on his face that said, rescue me. I remembered Min coming home from a party, wasted and pale and skinny but really alive-looking, glowing, at the same time. It was her Bowie period. I said something like oh, it's the thin white dude, and she'd said *duke*, Hattie, *duke*. Okay? Try to remember. She'd sounded so tired but she'd been sweet about it, patient, and had stayed up for a few minutes telling me about her party, about all the crazy things that had happened and how life was such a gas, a mustard gas.

—

So Thebes agreed to watch TV with the volume up high while Logan and I talked privately in the bathroom. She was watching the movie *Run Lola Run* and had decided to run *with* Lola, on the spot, in the gap between the beds, and see if she could keep up with her. Logan sat on the counter in the bathroom and played with the taps while I sat on the edge of the tub. I remembered Thebes's advice.

I felt pretty fucked up when I was fifteen, I said. I had a lot of secrets, you know, not secrets but things I couldn't tell anyone.

Yeah? said Logan.

And if you need to talk to someone, I'm here, you know, I'll listen to you, I said.

Yeah, he said.

I love you, I said, and Thebes loves you, and so does Min. Like crazy. You know that, right? I thought about saying something like *we've got to stick together, through good times and bad, blood is thicker than water,* something, anything to convince him that he wasn't alone in the world, but I knew he wouldn't buy it.

Yeah, he said.

I said we all acted like jerks sometimes when we were overwhelmed. Logan said he wasn't overwhelmed. I said, Okay, good, but we can see each other through stuff like that. Or even if we can't, it's just nice to know we want to, right?

Yeah, he said.

I told him he didn't have to put on an act for anybody, though, he didn't have to pretend he was in a great mood. Just that it might be good to talk about stuff sometimes.

Mmm-hmm, said Logan.

Hey, you know, I said, when I was fifteen I'd stay in my room for hours and hours at a time playing "A Whiter Shade of Pale" on my guitar and feeling completely misunderstood and unloved and stupid and ugly and fucked up and lonely. So phenomenally lonely. You know? I felt like the Little Prince. Totally, abjectly, alone on the planet. I mean, seriously, other people? Talking to them was like talking to a vapour or something. You know? I mean, there was no connection. There was . . . like, I was Robinson Freaking Crusoe. The Little Prince was totally alone on some planet, wasn't he?

You played what? asked Logan.

"A Whiter Shade of Pale," I said.

I think he had a flower, said Logan.

We were quiet for a while. Logan turned the taps on and off a few times. I checked out the ugly design on the shower curtain. Together we took big breaths.

And you know, I said, I'm probably the very last person in the world with the authority to talk about this stuff, but like, with girls and drugs and stuff like that? You'll be careful, right? Like, you'll be smart about that stuff, right?

Logan examined the ceiling tiles.

I mean, I know, you know, you're fifteen and it's sometimes, I don't mean to sound patronizing, but it's, at fifteen, a boy is, well girls too, I mean, you know, everyone . . . but they're . . . they are soo . . . *what the hell was I doing?* . . . horny. Right? You don't have to answer that. And it's hard, like impossible really, to think before, you know, jumping into something that seems really great at the time . . . in that particular moment . . . um.

Please, dear God, make Thebes have something bizarre and urgent that she's got to get off her chest right now. Bring her to this bathroom door, make her bang on it. Now, God, now!

Yeah, said Logan.

Can I ask you a question? I said.

Yeah.

How do you feel about this whole, you know, odyssey?

Odyssey?

Like, this trip we're on. What are you thinking?

Um, I don't know, he said. Fine?

Okay, but are you just saying that because you think that's what I want to hear?

Uh, sort of . . . I guess . . . I don't know.

So you're sort of feeling fine and sort of feeling something other than fine?

Maybe.

And what is the thing other than fine that you're feeling?

I don't know.

Well, is it scared? Or nervous?

I don't know.

Okay, but like right now if I had a gun to your head and you had to blurt out one thing you were feeling, like in order to save your life, or, say, Min's life, what would that one thing be, that one word? *Okay, super, so now I'm creating an imaginary scenario in which I hypothetically threaten his life and the life of his mother unless he speaks. Real cool. Real Barbara Coloroso.*

Can it be two words? he said.

Yes! I said. It can be as many words as you want. Let's talk all night!

Okay, um, let's see, he said. Four words.

And they are . . .

Really, really, really angry, he said.

I tried to get more out of him, but he shook his head and said he was also really, really, really tired. He looked like he was going to cry. I said okay, I understood. I did. It all made sense. It was normal. It was. I started to leave, and then he said, But who would just do that?

Do what? I said.

Like, just leave. You know? Like, just disappear.

You mean Cherkis? I said.

Logan pulled his hoodie over his face.

I don't know, I said. I really . . . you know . . . I just don't know. If we find him you can ask him, right? Maybe he thought it was the best thing . . . I don't know. Human beings . . .

Logan laughed for a second and sighed, then laughed again, just a gasp of air.

I know, I said. I'm an idiot. I don't know why I said "human beings." Lame. I'm just trying to—

Yeah, said Logan. No.

What, no? I said.

You're not an idiot, he said.

Well, actually, yeah, I really am, I said. Certified.

Whenever the clock says it's 11:11, said Logan, I automatically, without thinking, wish that Mom is happy.

Oh yeah. That 11:11 thing, I said, when stars crash into each other.

And then I always worry that I'm wasting another wish, he said.

Well, but, I said, it isn't like—

Sometimes I comfort myself, he said.

Really? You do?

Yeah, he said.

How? I said.

Sometimes I comfort myself by saying that every day, for as long as I live, will be either a Monday, Tuesday, Wednesday, Thursday, Friday, Saturday or Sunday.

I smiled. Whatever gets you through the night, I said.

He smiled back.

See? I said. Isn't this nice? This talking thing?

Yeah, he said. My tremendous people skills . . . Hey, why didn't you tell me I have two huge zits on my right cheek? He stared at his reflection.

What do you mean? I asked. You do have people skills . . .

Yeah, whatever, he said, and then started making faces in the mirror and riffing about his skills. If it weren't for these skills, he said, I don't know where I'd be. Sometimes my skills are so good they just intimidate people into not talking to me. And then I get nervous about using my terrific skills in front of people, so I mainly just act like I'm from a different culture.

Hey, I said, you know, sorry, but those two zits are only half the story.

What? he said. He got up really close to the mirror and peered at his face. Fuck, man! he said. Can you give me a minute alone in here?

No, you should leave them alone, I said. Scars.

He sat down on the toilet and crossed his legs and his arms and looked at me. Like if there was something about scars I could tell him that he didn't already know I could just go ahead and give it my best shot.

I didn't know what else to say. I had wanted Logan to understand that Cherkis hadn't decided one morning on a whim to leave his family, to blithely take off for something better and more exciting and leave his kids confused and angry and sad, but that in fact Min had forced him to leave. But I also didn't want Logan to be angry with Min for making Cherkis go away. Cherkis had tried hard to ride the tsunami waves of Min's moods and he'd managed for quite a long time, way longer than my parents and I had ever hoped for. Min resented his care, in the same way that she hated mine and anybody else's. But what were the people who loved her supposed to do? Tell her to go right ahead and starve herself, no big whoop, whatever, we don't care if you disintegrate right before our eyes. Yeah, polish off that giant bottle of sleeping pills all at once, do it, we can use the container for something else. How do you love someone who wants to be left alone to die? How do you stay? How do you walk away? My old Paris apartment is filled with psychology textbooks but I still haven't found the answer. There were two things I wanted and they were entirely incompatible. I wanted Min never to lose her children, to always have them nearby. And also, I wanted to tell Logan to set himself free, to live his life, not to worry about Min, he couldn't fix her, and he shouldn't feel guilty. But I didn't say any of that.

Hey, I said.

Yeah? said Logan.

You know Cherkis tried so hard to stay.

Yeah? said Logan.

I tried hard to stay too, I said.

He didn't say anything.

You might not understand, I said. Or, do you?

I don't know, said Logan.

I gave Logan an awkward hug and nearly knocked him into the sink. He told me I was stronger than I looked. He said he was going to have a shower.

I went into the other room and saw Thebes running like crazy, breathing hard, purple hair bobbing up and down as she tried to keep up with Lola. She saw me and bounded over and put her hands on my hips and locked her laser eyes on mine.

How did it go? she whispered.

Good, good, shhh, I said. You can stop running now.

No, she said. She was going to go all the way with Lola and save that guy's life.

eight

WE GOT UP EARLY THE NEXT MORNING, ate some
fruit from the cooler and loaded up the van. I stared at
the pool of something that was seeping out from under-
neath it. Logan had started playing Frisbee with Thebes
in the parking lot. He threw the Frisbee hard every time
against the pavement so it would deflect and fly up
straight into Thebes's hands. Or face. She didn't like it.

She kept yelling, Throw it normally, throw it normally! I looked around to make sure nobody was watching and then I got down on my hands and knees and stuck my finger in the mystery liquid and tasted it. I'd seen my father do this once or twice. Except I didn't really know what I was supposed to be tasting or how to differentiate it from any other automotive flavour. I decided it was water and not oil. It was water from the air conditioner, probably. I thought hey, excellent, we'll have to stop using the AC and open all the windows and the wind and the racket will drown out Thebes and muffle Logan's music. I didn't mind listening to Thebes's chatter or Logan's music most of the time, but I was trying to solve problems and formulate solutions in my mind and I needed to concentrate for a while. We were headed for Denver, and then we'd blast our way like amyl nitrate west through the Rocky Mountains.

I had this dream last night, said Logan. About a poet who finds out that his new book has no words, only thick blue ceramic-tile pages.

Was the poet Cherkis? I asked.

It wasn't clear, he said.

Logan complained about the birds waking him up. He said it wasn't even real singing, just *crawk, crawk, crawk*. I told him that male birds have to send warnings to other birds to stay off their turf and away from their mates, and Logan said he wasn't interested in their mates, all he wanted was to sleep. He yawned and wiped away a tear.

And this is fucked up, he said, but I also dreamt that I'd had a baby.

So did I! I said. The other night.

Logan rubbed his face and moaned and stared out the window. He didn't want to be having the same dreams and dark desires as his flabby-armed aunt.

How did you feel being pregnant? I asked him.

I don't know, he said. Distorted and inhabited.

Oh, okay, so you *do* know, I said.

I'd prefer to be the father in that type of scenario, he said.

All it means, I think, I said, is that we're expecting something.

Whatever, he said.

Min had told me a story about when Logan was a newborn baby. The guy in the apartment right next to hers, a Lithuanian philosophy professor, electrocuted himself in his bathtub and his body wasn't found for days and on the day that they discovered it Min had come in from a walk with Logan and she had cried and cried, thinking of the poor guy next door, and also how it was a terrible thing to come home with a newborn baby to an old guy having killed himself right next door. This old guy's mom had Alzheimer's and lived just down the hall in a different apartment and when he was alive she'd go banging on Min's door calling out for her son and thinking Min's apartment was his and then he or Min would patiently take her back to her own apartment. Somebody came and moved her away shortly after her son killed himself, but for a while there she'd still come banging on Min's door looking for him, calling out his name.

Soon after that there was a massive blizzard, the storm of the century they called it, when Cherkis was trapped in a restaurant and Min was alone with Logan and he was twelve days old and all the apartment windows were completely iced up so that it seemed like they were living inside a crystal, or a Christmas ornament, and there was nothing for Min to do but nurse Logan and hold him and take pictures of him and stare at him and listen to *True Stories* by the Talking Heads and teach herself how to juggle with the tiny Pampers diapers she'd roll up real tightly into balls after Logan had peed in them.

I thought about telling all that to Logan. Maybe Min already had. Or maybe you don't want to hear that right after being born you came home to a dead guy next door. I didn't know if that was the sort of thing Logan would think was mildly interesting, colourful, or just a really bad omen. Conversing with children is a fine art, I realized. An art form that demands large amounts of both honesty and misdirection. Or maybe *discretion* is a better word. Or a gradual release of information like time-controlled vitamins. Either way, my own befuddled attempts were pathetic and I really wanted to have more than odd, cryptic conversations with Logan and Thebes.

My mother and I were at Min and Cherkis's apartment before they brought Logan home from the hospital. Min and Cherkis were young, barely twenty years old, and their apartment was a mess. My mom made

Swedish meatballs and washed all of their dishes and cleaned the bathroom. I set up the baby mobile above Logan's crib and ran up and down four flights of stairs to do their laundry. When they got in, we all crowded around Logan and stared at him and whispered our compliments and beautiful wishes for their fantastic future together. Cherkis held Logan close to his chest— he'd taken his shirt off so Logan could feel his beating heart—and carried him from room to room telling Logan this is the living room, and this is the kitchen, and, buddy, this is the bedroom where you'll sleep. He took down a photograph he'd taken of a bleeding, screaming punk band because he thought it would disturb Logan and mess up his chi.

We all had some champagne, except for Min, who didn't want Logan getting drunk on her breast milk, and then Min and Cherkis lay down with Logan between them and my mom put out the incense they'd left burning in the living room and I bent over and kissed them all good night and then my mom came back into the bedroom and also kissed them all good night and then we left.

Did you know, said Thebes, that there's a shrine in Tokyo, in this park, Yoyogi Park, where you can buy a charm against all evil. *All* evil!

No, I didn't, I said.

And did you know that there's this really tiny building somewhere in Colombia, or maybe Ecuador, that is the official world headquarters of the Department of Unanswered

Letters. To work there it's mandatory that you have a history of killer depression, but I don't think—

Is that supposed to be a joke or what? said Logan.

Why, do you think depression is funny? said Thebes.

No, but I'm just saying . . . the way you delivered it sounded like a joke.

Depression's not a joke, yo, said Thebes.

I know it's not a joke, said Logan. I said the way you told that anecdote sounded like you were . . . like it was supposed to be a joke. Forget it.

Hey, said Thebes. How did you know that was air conditioner fluid?

I tasted it, I said.

Logan looked at me and frowned. That might have seemed like a really good idea at the time, he said, but maybe you should have taken a minute or even possibly two minutes to think about what you were doing.

I told you I wasn't qualified to be talking about that stuff, I said. Logan smiled and it was like . . . I don't know what it was like. A hurricane. Childbirth. Heroin. It rocked my world for a few seconds.

Hey, said Thebes, I read something about miners drinking their own urine in order to—

I read that too, said Logan.

Well, then, said Thebes, you know to mix it with tree bark, right? So the uric acid is killed? If you get stuck in an underground mine that's what you have to do.

There aren't any trees down there, genius, said Logan.

Well, Stephen Hawking, said Thebes, experienced miners bring their own bark just in case.

And then an animal jumped in front of our van and we hit its rear end and went skittering off the road, spun around and landed backwards in the ditch, but right side up.

What the fuck just happened? said Logan.

We hit a deer, said Thebes. I think it was a deer. Hattie, you killed it!

Are you serious? said Logan.

Oh my god, said Thebes. I can't believe we hit a deer. Why didn't you stop?

I didn't see it at all, I said. It was just there.

Oh my god, said Thebes.

Holy fuck, said Logan.

Are you guys okay? I said.

They said yeah and then we got out of the van and wandered down the highway a ways to see if the deer was still alive but it was lying in the middle of the road and there was blood everywhere and it looked dead. Its eyes were open. I picked up a small stone from the shoulder and slid it gently across the pavement. It hit the deer but the deer didn't blink or move. Thebes started to cry, she said she was now *impeccably* sad, and Logan put his arm around her shoulder.

We have to get him out of the middle of the road, I said.

Thebes said she couldn't touch him. Why did he do that? she said. I mean, like, why?

They just do, I told her. They don't get traffic.

Logan and I walked over to the deer and grabbed its hind legs and dragged it to the side of the road. Thebes didn't want to leave the deer, but I told her I'd call someone from the next gas station, some wildlife officer, and they'd take the deer away. There was blood and clumps of fur on the front bumper of the van and a big dent. Logan tried to get the blood off by throwing water on it from the cooler but it didn't really work, it just turned streaky. Then when I tried to start the van the ignition fell right out of the steering column and I had to use a screwdriver to get it going. Logan picked up the ignition for a closer look and I noticed that his hands were shaking slightly.

Are you okay? I asked him.

Yeah, totally, he said. You?

Well, I'm a little freaked out, I said. We just hit a deer.

Thebes couldn't stop crying.

Hey, T., said Logan, do you wanna play Hangman? You can start.

They played for a long time and Logan played by all of Thebes's goofy rules and she finally stopped crying and cheered up and Logan climbed back over into the front seat.

Logan was writing or drawing something. Is that a sketch-book? I asked him.

No, he said. It was a black, hardcover notebook with blank, unlined pages. Some of the pages had sketches on them. It looks exactly like a sketchbook, I said.

Mmm, he said.

It is a sketchbook, said Thebes. He doesn't want people to know about it though.

You mean like your song lyrics? I asked her.

Shut up! she said, and dropped back.

Logan read something out loud, something his art teacher had written about one of his sketches. *Logan,* she'd written, *this is an assignment tailor-made for your particular strengths . . . weird but fascinating creatures/shapes . . . very dreamlike.*

On the outside of his notebook he had a bunch of strange drawings and odd numbers. He read those to me too.

380 off the dribble
220 off the dribble
80 2 dribble
80 crossover
200 free throws
Ideal: 30 ft., 300 off the dribble, 500 3s, 150 mid-range
Ball handling
Weight, running, jumping
20 wind sprints over 90 minutes
BALL MOVEMENT
Take it to the cup
Fuck the People
Darkleaf

What was that last part? I asked him.

My music, he said.

They say we should wear goggles, said Thebes. The wind is that strong today. She was reading the newspaper. Then she was quiet for a minute. What do you guys think about setting yourself on fire as a means of protest? she asked. Quiet for another minute. We didn't bother to answer.

Okay, Hattie, she said, you're a Gemini and that's an air sign, which means you live more in your head than in your heart and you should try to remember and understand that all of humanity is interconnected and you should also try to be at one with the world and know that if you hurt somebody you're also hurting yourself.

Got it, I said, although I thought it would be easier to light myself on fire.

I pulled into a gas station and told the guy behind the counter that I'd hit a deer about ten miles back and it was lying dead on the side of the road and asked if he could call someone to have it taken away. He said yeah and asked me if there was any damage to the vehicle and I said yeah, but just a big dent, and the ignition fell out.

The ignition fell out? he said.

Yeah, but I can start it with a screwdriver, I said.

He said well, okay, fine, but if the impact had loosened up the ignition so it fell out then maybe other things would start falling off too, and I said, okay, thanks, we'll watch out for them, and we left.

So, we're in a boat, said Logan. This was a dream he had had a few nights ago. And, yeah, he said, we're just in it floating around in the ocean, and then Grandpa comes up and he's smiling, this big, huge smile, and, you know, we're all hauling him into the boat and he says, Man, am I happy to see you guys! He had a moustache, said Logan.

No, he didn't have a moustache, I said. Logan hadn't ever actually seen his grandpa.

Well, in my dream he did, he said.

I wanted Logan to keep talking about his dreams and his sketchbook or anything else at all.

Read me this, I said. I handed him his CD case. I wanted to hear his voice so I could remember its exact tone and timbre when I was back in Paris hunting down my boyfriend. So I'd be able to hear Logan saying to me, *Jesus, Hat, give it up, man, fuck.* But then when he actually did talk it was a question that took me by surprise.

Hey, he said, were you around when Mom first went off the deep end?

No, I said.

No? he said. Well, where were you?

Well, I mean, yeah, I said. I mean, I guess so.

And? he said.

She'd gone out late one evening in February to have a nap under a tree in the field behind the giant Discount Everything store a few blocks from our house. It was so cold our pipes froze that night. It was my job to thaw them out. I had to wrap them up in blankets and then sit on the floor using a hair dryer to blow hot air on them. A barrel fuse blew that night too, and I had to rummage around in the dark with a flashlight.

I remember peering over the fuse box saying, stove, fridge, dryer, stove, fridge, dryer, over and over, trying to figure it out. It was a record cold night, minus fifty-something with a deadly wind chill. Our house was shaking, none of our doors would close, and empty pizza boxes were flying past our windows. It was the kind of night where if you froze to death they'd have had to set up a tent around your body with giant industrial heaters in it, just to be able to peel you off the ground. Even the cool kids were walking backwards down the street to keep the wind from killing them. It was snowing horizontally and the streets all over the city were buckling and collapsing and swallowing up traffic.

It's so beautiful, Min said when they found her under that tree. She said she'd seen an airplane explode in the air and crash. The cops said later that she'd almost frozen to death but not quite. She'd been out there for two and a half hours. One of them said she was shaking hands with God.

So she had to go to the hospital for a few weeks.

When she came home she thought her fingers would have to be cut off and then her hands and then even her arms, right above the elbow. She said she wouldn't even be able to wipe her own ass. Nothing we could say would convince her that she was fine, that nothing would be amputated, and then one day she started doing it herself, cutting deep rivets into her wrists, getting it over with, and she had to go back to the hospital for quite a long time.

When she got home, our mother slept with her at night, in Min's bed, and sometimes I'd curl up at their feet or on the floor in front of her door so she wouldn't run away. When she was well enough to leave the house I'd follow her. She'd walk for miles sometimes, never stopping at a friend's place or a store or a park or anything at all, just walking, quickly, and staring at her feet or off into the middle distance. One evening I had convinced her not to go for a walk. I begged her to stay at home and play gin rummy with me and she agreed to, and she made us milkshakes and popcorn and she told me that she had known that I'd been following her and that she wasn't angry about it but that I didn't have to do it any more.

Are you afraid I'll do something stupid? she asked me, and I said yeah, I was, and she promised me she wouldn't, although she really couldn't understand why I would care, and I told her because I loved her, and she smiled and shook her head like I was a complete fool.

Logan had carved *Don't take this the wrong way* into the dashboard.

Don't take what the wrong way? I asked him.

Just, you know what, he said. Try not to be so literal.

Thebes popped up from the back. Where's North America again? she asked.

Oh my god, said Logan. He shrank into his hoodie.

nine

SO, WE WERE WHISTLING SOUTH ALONG THE I-25 and Logan was looking at the map. I want to go to Moab, he said. Moab, Utah.

Why? I asked.

I don't know.

What is that again? I said. Moab.

He shrugged. No clue, he said.

I think it's from the Bible, I said. It's a people. Moabites or . . .

Mother of All Bombs, said Logan.

No, I said. Well, yeah, but . . . Or it's a place . . . in Jordan? Egypt? Moab. Hmmm.

Moab, said Thebes. Bastard son of Lot. Moab, said Thebes. An ancient region by the Dead Sea, or its people. Etymology of Moab, she said. A corruption of "seed of a father" or as a participial form from "to desire," thus connoting "the desirable land."

Thanks, Thebes, I said.

The Holy Rashi in Humash, said Thebes, explains the word *Moav* to mean "from the father" since "av" in Hebrew means "father."

Great, Thebes, thanks, I said.

Fritz Hommel, said Thebes, regards *Moab* as an abbreviation of "Immo-ab," which means "his mother is his father."

Thebes, thank you.

Just helping a brother out, she said, and slammed her dictionary shut.

So, yeah, let's go there, said Logan.

Thebes, I said, do you want to?

I'm down, she said. Where is it?

Logan was still studying the map. Hey, he said, if we went to Moab we could check out Mexican Hat and Tuba City. They're kind of on the way to the Painted Desert.

Are they towns? asked Thebes.

Yeah, he said. I guess so. Concept towns or something.

———

When Logan was a baby Min would tie him up in a bike seat with an old scarf and then they'd ride all over the city. Sometimes he'd fall asleep, and wearing this huge kid's bike helmet he looked like an extraterrestrial, and it would thump against her back and she'd have to reach around and prop it up and hold it there, his giant, oversized head, while she rode around with one hand. She put him to sleep under tables in cafés, on friends' couches, in fields at rock concerts. She took him everywhere. When he was four he'd get up really early in the morning and make calls to people he knew, like me, to see how we were doing and to tell us about his morning.

Hey, I said, remember how much Min hated your kindergarten teacher?

Yeah, he said. His kindergarten teacher had called Min up and told her that he was concerned that Logan didn't know how to stand on one foot and that he didn't know his colours.

That was crap, Min had said. He'd been hopping on one foot since he was a year old and knew his colours at two. She asked the teacher if maybe Logan was just being funny in a five-year-old way when he said blue was red or whatever, or maybe he just didn't feel like hopping around on one foot, why should he? Then the teacher told Min that he'd send Logan, this tiny kid who had just barely started school, to the principal's office if he didn't cooperate with the testing thing. So Min had said okay, as soon as he did that he should call her because she'd have his ass fired at the very same time.

And then Logan told me this story about how one day, long after he was out of kindergarten, like when he was eleven or twelve, he and Min had seen that teacher waiting at a bus stop when they were walking home from the grocery store and Min started hopping around him on one foot and saying all kinds of goofy things like oh, look, it's very important to be able to do this. Can you do this? Because if you are not able to hop on one foot you may as well kill yourself. Nobody will hire you. Nobody will marry you. Nobody will want to be your friend. She went on and on.

I had to beg her to stop, said Logan.

She was still pissed after all those years, eh? I said.

That's a long time to be mad, said Logan.

Then I told Logan about something else he'd done when he was four or five. Min had asked me to take him to his Orff class at the conservatory. It was the first one and the teacher had gone around the room asking their names. Logan said his name was Logan "I don't wanna be here" Troutman.

Yeah, he said, he vaguely remembered that. He hadn't felt like doing that Orff stuff either.

So, yeah, I said, while the other kids were dinging the triangle or knocking some pieces of wood together, you were lying on the floor doing this seal act, rocking on your chest with your arms behind your back going *orf, orf, orf*.

I used to be cute, he said. Adoptable.

Oh, c'mon, I said. You're still adoptable. It was supposed to be a joke, but it was a stupid one given the
circumstances.

Thebes popped up. See, she said, Logan did funny,
clever things and all I liked to do was lie in the sandbox
and have a nice, long crap in my diaper and then fall asleep
in the sun. Min said it was my favourite thing. Like I was
some rat or wino or something.

You were a contented kid, I said.

Not that ambitious, said Logan.

But really, he said, who adopts fifteen-year-old boys?

Well, I said, I guess, yeah . . . not many people.

They go into group homes, said Logan.

Or foster homes, I said. But only until they're
eighteen.

And then? asked Logan.

Well, I said, they go wherever. They do their thing.
They're adults then.

Hey, said Thebes. She punched Logan in the arm.
Remember when you burst that blood vessel in your eye
from vomiting so hard when you got drunk with your
basketball team?

I still have it, he said. He opened his left eye wide and
looked at Thebes.

Dude! she said. You should wear a patch. I'll make
you one.

They went on like that for a while. I was happy they
were talking. Remembering. Reminiscing about their
childhood, like it hadn't all been one long march to the
frozen Gulag.

But, said Logan, a fifteen-year-old could technically live on his own, right?

Okay, bad times are gonna roll, I thought. Logan is planning to run away before we find Cherkis.

No, a fifteen-year-old cannot live on his own, I said.

Pippi Longstocking wasn't even fifteen, said Thebes, and she—

Yeah, but she was a character in a book, I said.

And she was Swedish, said Logan.

So there would have been a solid safety net of social programs to help keep her afloat, I said. It doesn't work here.

Yeah, but the point of Pippi was that she didn't need anybody or any social programs to help her, said Logan. She was that strong.

Yeah, I said, but unhumanly so. She could lift a horse. Can you?

Well, I don't know, said Logan. A small one, maybe, but that's not my point. There was more to her strength than that. It was—

You could so *not* lift a horse, said Thebes.

Yeah, I probably could, said Logan.

No, you couldn't, she said. But I could probably flip a horse.

I could *eat* a horse, said Logan.

Oh, the things they could do to horses. They ping-ponged back and forth for a long time about horses and tough Swedish girls while I looked for a gas station and/or grocery store.

———

Min was married briefly to a grip a few years ago, long after Cherkis had hit the road. The grip's name was Darius. They met on a movie set. Min was working as a driver, or maybe as a caterer. I wasn't sure. When the shooting was finished, they drove down to Vegas to spend Min's wages on blackjack. The plan was that if she and Darius made enough money from blackjack they would get married at the Elvis chapel, for the hell of it.

Logan didn't care what they did. Min told me that he spent the entire time in Vegas in front of the cracked bathroom mirror of the hotel room perfecting his Robert De Niro impersonation and trying to get the family thrown out of as many casinos as he could.

Min and Darius chose package B, which included a limo to pick them up and drop them off, a medley of Elvis tunes by the impersonator, some flowers, a videotape of the wedding, and a guy named Juan to be the minister. Is it real or what? Darius asked Min. Of course it's real, she told him. Not that she really cared. She didn't care about being married to anyone, she just wanted to be loved. But she didn't want to be taken care of. Or she did. She told me that Thebes had taken her hand and crammed it into Darius's. She wore a dress that was red on the top and then gradually faded into light orange at the very bottom.

When they got home Darius lived with them for a while, but then decided that what he really needed for his personal growth was to get rid of his possessions and take a very long, indefinite trip to the North Pole. That's great, Min said. She was tired of having all that self-esteem anyway. Blech. Feeling good was lousy for her art.

They said goodbye to Darius. He told Min she shouldn't take it personally, that she had taught him so much about love, and he told Thebes he'd send her a Christmas present straight from Santa's workshop. *Right, right.* He and Logan had nothing to say to each other.

Denver was coming up any minute but we decided to bypass it and veer off west on the I-70 towards the mountains, and the desirable land of Moab. Logan was reading a new *Q* magazine he'd bought at the last gas station. Thebes was reading over his shoulder.

Hattie, she said, your boyfriend, Ryan Adams, is two-timing you with Winona Ryder.

I just said I liked his music, sort of, I said.

She told me her last assignment in school, before she was sprung, had been to research the life of an important individual in musical history.

Who did you do? I asked her.

Beyoncé Knowles, she said, from Destiny's Child.

What do you think the odds are of me ever achieving knighthood? said Logan.

Oh, I said, sixteen to one, around there.

What do you have to do to be knighted? asked Thebes.

I don't know, said Logan, something great.

Okay, here we go, I said. I pulled into a gas station and up to the pump.

Thebes wanted to pump the gas. She jumped out of the van with a karate kick and almost smashed into the other guy pumping gas. He looked at her like he was about to be assaulted by Happy the dwarf.

I don't know, said Logan, but I think Thebes is starting to smell bad. I told him it was very considerate of him not to have mentioned it when she was around. I asked him if it was my job to get her to shower or bathe and he said he had no idea. He thought yeah, probably, and that she would need aggressive encouragement because it wasn't really her thing. He got out of the van and suddenly there were about six Japanese teenagers standing around him. They pointed at his headphones and smiled. He smiled back at them.

Rock 'n' roll? one of them said.

Yeah, said Logan. Rock 'n' roll.

Rock 'n' roll! said the guy.

Yes! said Logan. Rock 'n' roll.

They were all smiling and feeling groovy. I told Logan I wanted to use the pay phone to call Min and he said he wanted to talk to her too.

The hospital said Min wasn't available. Oh, I said, what exactly does that mean? They asked if they could phone me back later in the day, after rounds. No, see, I said, the thing is I'm at a pay phone. Can I phone *you* later?

What are they saying? said Logan.

Well . . . not much, I whispered.

Ask to speak to Min, he said.

I did, I said. I can't right now.

Can you just tell me in a nutshell how she's doing? I asked the woman. Thebes was wandering around the parking lot looking at the ground and occasionally bending down and picking things up.

Well, said the woman, there have been a few incidents and she's—

What kind of incidents? I asked. Logan looked at me. It's okay, it's okay, I whispered to him.

She's not adapting to the program the way we would have liked her to, said the woman.

Oh yeah? I said. So, what does that mean? She's fine, I whispered to Logan. Stupidly gave him two thumbs way up.

Well, she's somewhat hostile towards the nurses, said the woman. And her roommate. And her doctor. She refuses to speak. She won't eat. She won't get out of bed. Not for any reason.

Oh, that's not . . . that's unfortunate, I said. The woman agreed.

She's good, she's good, I said to Logan. Is she okay? I asked the woman.

The woman said yes, she'd been sedated and was resting. She couldn't say much more than that but if I could call back, after rounds, she was sure the doctor could tell me more.

All right, okay, I said. I lowered my voice and asked the woman if Min had indicated any interest at all in seeing me or her kids.

Not that she knew of, said the woman. In fact, she said, one nurse had told her that Min had said she'd never had children.

Okay, I said. Can you just tell me exactly at what time I'd be able to speak to her doctor?

No, she couldn't, she said, it varied, it depended on how many patients the doctor was seeing and how long it would take for him to see them. Et cetera, she added.

But ballpark, I said. I had developed a killer headache in the last five seconds. I put my hand on Logan's shoulder. I felt like I was going to fall. I could hear Thebes singing something over by the Free Air. She was twirling around, fully inhabiting her weird zone, lit up by the sun and laughing.

You okay? said Logan.

Of course! I said.

I'm sorry, said the woman, I wish I could tell you more. Really, it would be best if you could call again later. Tell me your name again? In case I'm able to pass the message on to the patient . . .

Min! I said. I mean, no, Hattie! Hattie Troutman. I'm Min's sister. *What the fuck?*

I hung up and smiled. Okay! I said. Everything's fine. Gold. She's busy.

She's busy? said Logan. Doing what?

Oh, stuff . . . like, you know, I said. They have meals and then they have Group and then they have sessions and then . . . tests . . . They walk around too, don't they? It's nuts.

Well, he said, why'd you ask if she was okay?

I don't know, I said. No, I do know. Because that's obviously the big question, right? Is she okay? I mean, that's what we want to know, right? That's why we're calling the hospital. I sat down on the pavement and leaned against the cinder-block wall of the gas station. I closed my eyes and tried to pray but all I could do was channel

Bowie and think about how planet Earth was blue and there was nothing I could do.

What are you—Are you okay? asked Logan. He crouched down beside me.

Oh, yeah, I said. It's just so hot . . . isn't it?

When I came to I was stretched out in the supply room with a fan blasting cold air five inches from my face and Logan and Thebes sitting cross-legged on the concrete floor beside me, staring. I looked at the kids and smiled.

Wassup, player? said Thebes.

Thebes, said Logan. Jesus.

I showed Logan how to start the van with the screwdriver. If you get pulled over, tell them you're sixteen, I said.

What do I do if they ask to see my driver's licence? he said.

Oh, I don't know, I said. Stall for time. Don't get pulled over.

He'd drive to a town called Fruita and then we'd deke down to Moab. First of all he stopped at a grocery store and he and Thebes ran in and bought some cheese and salami and something she called shabu-shabu and bread and fruit and water and a bunch of jumbo-sized chocolate bars and fireworks and a stylin' cover with flames on it for the steering wheel and a bottle of wine for me and a corkscrew.

I lay in the back seat of the van and listened to a family in the parking lot discussing our licence plate.

What the hell is that? said the guy.

It's not what, it's where, honey, said the woman. It's a licence plate.

Yeah, said the guy, but what the hell does it say?

It says something like Anaconda, said the woman, or . . .

No, it doesn't, it says . . . lemme see.

The guy slapped his hand on the back window and I sat up and opened the side door and said, It says Manitoba, okay? Manitoba.

Where the hell is that? said the guy. In California?

Yes, it is, I said.

Well, now, there you go, hon, mystery solved, said the woman.

When I opened up the bottle of wine, Thebes said whoa, you *yanked* that cork out of there like you were saving it from drowning. She got out her markers and drew a screaming face on the cork. She made me a sandwich and cut it into tiny triangles, bite-size. I lay on the back seat with my head in her lap and she tried to cheer me up. She made the rescued cork sing songs from *Super Fly* and she played games with me. Logan was driving with his mondo headphones on so his music wouldn't bug me but mostly so he couldn't hear Thebes.

Okay, said Thebes, who would you rather have as a boyfriend? Frankenstein or George Bush?

Frankenstein, I said.

Okay, who would you rather have as a boyfriend? Frankenstein or Freddie Krueger?

Frankenstein, I said.

Okay, who would you rather have as a boyfriend? Frankenstein or Peter Pumpkineater?

Peter Pumpkineater. No, wait, I said. Franken—

No, you already said Peter Pumpkineater, said Thebes. Who would you rather have as a boyfriend? Peter Pumpkineater or Snoop Dogg?

Snoop Dogg.

Okay, who would you rather have as a boyfriend? Snoop Dogg or Paul Martin?

We did that for a few minutes until I eventually ended up with the Lion King's runty brother as my boyfriend.

The whole time I was thinking about Min. Well, I was also thinking about Marc and I was thinking about Cherkis, and I was thinking about what a world-class champion of fucked-up I was. One week ago I'd been a carefree bon vivant in the City of Lights ballin' in the mad cheddar, as Thebes would say, and now I was passing out in gas stations and drinking wine out of the bottle with an imaginary animal for a boyfriend and a fifteen-year-old at the wheel. I didn't know if we should turn around and go back home, head straight to the hospital, or crank it up a notch and haul ass to Twentynine Palms. Maybe drive all night. But in which direction?

Thebes and I fell asleep all tangled up while Logan careened like a rangy demon through the mountains with his Biggie blasting and the wind howling and semi drivers blaring their horns at him to get the hell away from them.

ten

WHEN I WOKE UP we were in a corner of the parking lot of a motel, parked under a dim streetlight covered in moths. Logan was slumped, asleep, over the wheel and Thebes was lying on the floor, also asleep, between the back and the front seats. I sat up carefully and silently and looked at them. The streetlight was buzzing but not very loudly and some moths were gently throwing themselves against the windshield of the van. Logan was snoring very, very quietly and still gripping the wheel with both hands. His music had stopped. His notebook was in his lap. I reached around to the front and picked it up and stared at it. Logan had used a fat Sharpie to write *Hot Tears Is a Concept* on the cover. I put it back in his lap.

Thebes looked a little confused while she slept, like she was trying to remember what the distance was between the sun and the earth or why it was, again, that she'd had to be born. She had a thin moustache of sweat on her upper lip and her hair was plastered to her head. She had corked up my bottle of wine, and I meticulously uncorked it again and sat there sipping plonk and wondering what it would feel like to leave these two homies behind.

Hi, Hattie, whispered Thebes. Are you awake? Where are we?

Hey, I said. I don't know. Moab, probably. You okay?

Rock solid, she said. She glanced at Logan draped over the wheel. Did he get shot?

No, I said. He's sleeping.

She wiped her eyes and mouth with one filthy hand and patted my knee with the other one. Drinking alone? she said.

No, you're here, I said.

I don't count, she said. Want to hear my dream?

Yeah, I said. Tell me.

I dreamt that there was a thirteenth month, she said. And everybody knew about it except me. Like, it had been there all along, like all throughout time. A thirteenth month, and nobody had told me. And then I found out that even my birthday was in the thirteenth month, which was squeezed somewhere in between February and March. And this month, the thirteenth month, was called Shtetl. So, like, my birthday was Shtetl the Eighth.

Shtetl, I said.

Do you know what that is? she said. She was busy adjusting her holster.

No, I said, well, yeah, sort of. Like, a small town. I think it's a Hebrew word, like Moab. Maybe that's why you had the dream.

But I didn't know that word before my dream, said Thebes.

We tried to wake Logan up but it was impossible. He wouldn't budge.

Sure he hasn't been capped? said Thebes.

Yeah, I said, you can hear him snoring, can't you?

We decided to spend the night in the parking lot, in the van. We'd save some money, and the night was almost over anyway.

Cops came around at dawn, apparently—I didn't notice, I was sleeping—and they asked Thebes what we were doing there and she said sleeping and they said we weren't allowed to sleep there, it wasn't a campground, and the motel front-desk person was suspicious, and Thebes said okay, we'd leave, except that her peeps were still asleep, one at the wheel, and so what was she supposed to do?

They said all right, that was fine, we could sleep for a while. Better that than another exhausted motorist on the highway. They didn't ask to see Logan's licence. As soon as I opened my eyes a crack, Thebes was in my face.

Popo says when Lo wakes up we're outie, she said.

Thebes, I said. This talking thing? The way you talk, it's—

No, no, she said, shhh, please don't tell me how to talk. I have to do it this way, okay? I won't always. She looked like she was about to cry again so I told her no, no, it was fine, she could talk however she wanted, it was stupid of me to have brought it up, we were good.

Logan woke up. He moaned and swore and stretched and then slumped over the wheel again. Smells like ass in here, he said. Thebes and I said good morning and asked him if he knew where we were.

Moab, he said. He got out of the van and walked way over to some trees to pee and stood with his back to us for a few minutes. When he got back he rifled around in his fake alligator suitcase and pulled out a stick of incense and lit it and waved it around the van, mostly in Thebes's general direction. She whipped out one of her pistols and fired a few rounds at his head.

You die, hippie, she said.

We all agreed we'd drive around Moab, check out the sights, and have breakfast in a restaurant instead of eating soggy shabu-shabu sandwiches or whatever rotten fruit was bobbing around in the cooler. We ate at a dive, Logan's choice, called King Solomon's, in honour of Deborah Solomon, the love of his life. He'd bought a copy of *The New York Times* to see where she was at. I left the kids at the table to fight over the miniature jukebox

and gawk at Moabites while I wandered around the restaurant in search of a pay phone and a machine that might
sell Advil or Tylenol or morphine. I called the hospital
and got a hold of the same woman, oh, harbinger of grim,
at least I think it was the same woman, and asked if I
could speak with Min. She said no, she was sorry, it wasn't
possible, the doctor hadn't made his rounds, Min was in a
locked-down recovery room, there had been some trouble
that morning and, no, I couldn't speak to her.

Yeah, but, what the fuck! I said, and immediately
apologized. Silence on the other end. I'm sorry, I said. I'd
like to know if she's okay right now. And, also, what do
you mean, trouble? I'm sorry, again.

She's not in any immediate danger, said the woman.
I thought about Superman, her certified intrepid roommate, and wondered where she'd got to, what nemesis
she'd been busy battling, when Min had been in trouble.

Can you tell me what happened? I said.

You're family? said the woman. I just need to
confirm . . .

Yes, I said, my name's Hattie Troutman. I'm her sister.
I've been calling . . .

She disappeared for a short time, said the woman. She
was gone for about an hour and a half.

Where'd she go? I asked.

Well, she said she was going out for a cigarette, and—

But she doesn't smoke, I said.

Well, we didn't know that, said the woman.

And I thought you just said she wasn't getting out of
bed at all, so how did she—?

Well, that's true, she wasn't, so we were all quite encouraged by the fact that she had decided to get up for some fresh air. Well, a cigarette.

And then she just walked away or . . . ? I said.

Apparently, yes, she started walking towards the highway. The police picked her up and brought her back. But she is out of danger, like I said, added the woman.

Oh, Min, I thought. C'mon . . . c'mon!

If I was there, I said, at the hospital, would I be able to see her right now?

Honestly? said the woman.

Yeah! Yes, please!

The doctor has her on a range of meds, said the woman. We're working . . . we're trying to establish what it is she needs and what her body can tolerate. At this point if she were to have guests she'd probably not . . . She's not coherent, she's fairly agitated, she's refusing to eat . . . she's having difficulty remembering aspects of her life, her address, for instance, the names of her kids . . . I recall telling you earlier that at one point she insisted that she hadn't *had* kids.

Oh, you know, I said, I don't . . . Really? I actually can't believe that. I looked at the kids way over on the other side of the restaurant. Thebes had taken all her filthy, sweaty hair and sculpted it upwards like a Smurf's and stuck a Sharpie through it Pebbles Flintstone–style and even from that distance I could hear her say, Bro, what's a Lynyrd Skynyrd? Logan's head was on the table.

I know, said the woman, it's difficult. It's a stressful time for the family, but we have every reason to believe that Min will recover and very likely be back at home soon. Provided there's someone there to help out, or perhaps home care . . .

Every reason to believe, I said. I wondered what those reasons were, if there was a master copy I could get my hands on, the holy grail, if I could get all those reasons to believe tattooed onto my body and anchored to my brain. Every reason to believe. Maybe there was one single reason to believe, if that, but *every reason*? I'd seen Min in and out of enough hospitals to know they were bluffing, the medical staff. They had to sound hopeful, for everybody's sake, and I appreciated it, but I knew it wasn't true.

I thanked the woman for the information. I asked her to pass hugs and kisses on to Min from Logan and Thebes. Logan and Thebes, I repeated. Those are her kids. I didn't want to get off the phone with this woman because it meant going back to the table and being face to face with the forgotten ones. But the woman was angling for an exit and people were beginning to stare at Thebes and her Theban ways and I didn't want someone calling her a retard again.

We drove around the town for a while. Thebes and I dropped Logan off at a basketball court and went to find a store where we could buy her some new clothes.

I want them to be all white, she said.

Nooooo, I said. That is not a good choice for you.

But she really wanted them so I caved and said she could buy whatever clothes she liked.

And when we see Cherkis, she said, he can tie-dye them if he wants.

So, hey, Thebie, I said, how do you feel, are you looking forward to meeting him? We were having this conversation in the store. She was trying on clothes and I was sitting on the floor outside the change room door.

She was and she wasn't, she said, but wouldn't or couldn't elaborate other than to say she was trying to figure out the first thing that she would tell him.

I asked her if she wanted to rehearse it with me. She said no, she wanted it to sound fresh and spontaneous. Then she told me she had always harboured a secret desire to be an actress.

But, she said, I'm sort of depressed about it because I still don't have an agent.

I didn't know if she was serious or pretending to be a wannabe in L.A. commiserating with her friends at some audition. I didn't know if I should laugh or not.

Maybe Cherkis has connections in California, she said.

Maybe, I said. You never know. She burst out of the change room, all in white, all Hi ho, Silver, away! God, you scared me, I said.

What do you think? she asked. She spun around and did a few jumping jacks. She teetered around like Chaplin, twirling an imaginary cane.

You just . . . I don't know . . . You're beautiful, though. Definitely. Wow!

Does it totally work? she asked.

Yeah! I said. What do you call that colour? Vanilla?

Eggshell, she said.

So we left the store with Thebes wearing a little white double-breasted suit jacket and trousers, shirt, vest and tie.

You look like Hervé Villechaize, or I don't know . . . Tom Wolfe, I told her.

Who's that? she said.

Writer guy, I said.

Brother to Virginia?

No.

Have you read her diaries? she asked.

No.

Min has, she said.

That didn't surprise me. Virginia Woolf, Sylvia Plath, *Anna Karenina* . . . Min's girl guide to the universe of pain. Her library of loss. She was well read.

Thebes also bought some eggshell tank tops and eggshell terry cloth shorts and eggshell knee socks and eggshell Converse Chucks.

Then we went to find Logan at the basketball court. We got lost on the way, drove around in circles, and then finally remembered the name of the street it was on. When we got there Logan was talking to some cops. Not the same cops, according to Thebes, that had told us we couldn't sleep in the parking lot.

I jumped out of the van and went over there and asked them what was up. Logan was obviously in pain and the cops pointed at his wrist.

It's broken, they said. He won't tell us how it happened. His wrist dangled grotesquely from his arm and the cops said he'd have to get it plastered.

God, Logan, I said, are you okay?

Yeah, yeah, said Logan. His eyes were watering. Turned out that Logan had been hustling some of the kids at the court with his standard ten-for-eleven scam, pretending to suck at first to lure them in and make them put their money on the table.

How'd you break your wrist? I asked him. He shrugged. Whoever broke his wrist must have threatened him with something worse if he told anyone. Or, he broke it himself on another guy's face and wouldn't admit it. There was nobody else around.

The cops said if we left town immediately after he got a cast put on that thing, they wouldn't press any charges.

But what charges would you press? I asked. I mean, they're just kids, right? Playing?

Mischief, said one of the cops.

Yeah, but, what do you mean, mischief? I mean—

We don't want any trouble, said one of them.

Yeah, well, I understand that, I hate trouble too, but I mean—

We're actually trying to give you a break, here, said one of the cops. Are you always this mouthy?

I don't think I'm being *mouthy*, I said. I'm just trying to figure this out. I want some information. Like, what he'd actually be charged with . . . I'm just not clear on the nature of these so-called charges. You know?

The cops were very calm and actually quite reasonable. It was making me nuts. I wanted a fight too. I wanted to break my wrist on a stranger's head and scam some Moabites and get run out of town for being better at something than the other kids.

Okay, listen, said one of the cops. We're talking Fraud. We're talking Extortion. We're talking Illegal Gambling.

No, c'mon, gimme a break, you are not talking about those things, dude, I said. He's fifteen freaking years old! It's a stupid basketball game! What do you mean, extortion? That is so ridiculous. Do you make this shit up or what? What do you do, just drive around town busting kids for being kids? Thebes was tugging on my shirt and Logan was staring at me with a familiar combination of pain and pity, those cobalt eyes going off like alarms way deep in his hoodie. I reminded myself of my mother shorting out on everyone after my father drowned saving our lives.

The cops were quiet. They folded their arms and cocked their heads and looked at me.

Why don't the three of you just leave, ma'am, said one of them, not unkindly. He put his hand out like, *here's the way, go, we're letting you off.* Thebes and Logan started walking back to the van. I began to cry, stupidly. I asked them where the hospital was and they gave me directions and wished me well. They said Logan should join an after-school basketball program instead of hustling other kids.

Well, yeah, but he's been expelled, I said.

They understood. It happened. Boys. You know. One of them shook my hand empathetically and said he had a houseful of teenage boys waiting for him when he got off his shift.

Still got the green? asked Thebes when we were all back in the van.

Logan said no, the other guys had rolled him and taken his cash and his knife and his ball. Wicked outfit, T., he added.

At the hospital he got a cast and a lecture and a tetanus shot because he'd also cut his hand grabbing onto the rusty hoop after the dopest dunk, man, and the bill was seventy million bucks, or, I'm not sure, four hundred and ninety billion, and would be sent to Marc Babin at my old address in Paris. It was the only official address I had on my ID.

Coolio, said Thebes, let's roll. We got back into the van and she dove into the back seat, spelunking through her art supplies until she found her favourite indelible markers and pleading with Logan to let her beautify his cast.

There'd been a girl outside the hospital, smoking, and I'd joined her for a minute while Logan was getting his cast and Thebes was chatting with an orderly who was also dressed in white.

I didn't know exactly, but I think the smoking girl's friend had just OD'ed. The girl had leaned against the wall and closed her eyes. She'd looked so tired, so sad and messed up.

What do you think the chances are of everything being okay? she said. I told her I didn't know. I had no idea. Her guess was as good as mine. It was like I was having a conversation with myself and hadn't worried so much about being polite and hopeful because it was only me.

Now, as we were heading out of town, I felt bad. I had this urge to go back and find her and say something more consoling. I thought about what that might be.

I remembered Min after one of her unsuccessful suicide attempts waking up in the hospital, surrounded by me and our parents, and the only thing she said was, rats, dark ages. When she came home, our mother offered to give her a haircut but halfway through Min decided she hated having scissors snipping at her neck and ears and asked our mother to stop. For three months she had a bob that was six inches shorter on one side and even when she went back to school and kids made fun of her she pretended not to care.

Logan said he was going to do some work on his Robert Goulet project, just in case they ever let him back into his school. He didn't want to be so far behind that he'd be one of those guys, one of those grown men, with a beard and children and two ex-wives, crammed into a too-small desk trying to get his grade twelve.

We had to pick a Western Canadian historical figure, he said. He said he was writing a diary in Robert Goulet's voice, about his childhood and rise to fame. Did you know, he said, that when Robert Goulet was five years old, his family took a burnt cork and covered his face in "blackface" and watched him perform?

Thebes was drawing on Logan's cast. She drew a heart with his name and Deborah Solomon's in it. He made her change it.

She looked up something in her dictionary. I know, she said. I'll draw an ulna. She drew an ulna along the cast, and the other bone and joint parts of his arm and wrist and hand. Then she coloured it black all around that, so the white bony parts stood out and it looked pretty good, quite skeletal. She asked Logan if she could write two very short poems entitled "The Sunset" and "The Room" on the other side of his cast and he said yeah.

Min had once put me in a body cast, for a school art project. I'd been so eager and excited when she'd asked me to help her out. Our parents were away for the weekend and Min really relished being in charge.

I wore my bathing suit, and she slathered two giant jars of Vaseline that she'd bought onto my body, and then she stuck layers and layers of plaster on me and told me I'd have to wait for two hours until it had hardened and then she'd cut it off and I'd be free. She told me she had to zip out for a few minutes to buy something, but she didn't come back until the next day and I was left alone in the house in a body cast, unable to move. I stood in the middle of the living room for a long time, and then I tipped myself over onto the floor and lay there trying not to cry because I didn't want the salt in my tears to make me thirstier than I already was.

Please don't tell Mom and Dad, she said, when she finally returned. Or we'll never be left alone again. I promised I wouldn't but I didn't agree with her reasoning. I didn't think I wanted to be left alone with her again.

She cut the plaster off with a saw and several knives. It took hours and by the time she was finished I had tiny cuts all over my body and a bright red rash. It's perfect, she said, of the life-sized cast. It looks more like you than you.

———

The van was making strange sounds. Logan asked me if I'd heard it and I said yeah, but I was going to ignore it.

Well, he said, but you should listen to it carefully, like to the type of sound it is, so you can tell someone if we break down. Articulate the problem, he said. You know?

No, I said, I don't know. But you're right.

Thebes made me a gift certificate. It entitled me to have her keep up to ten secrets for me. She drew ten squares at the bottom that we could punch out with the hole puncher she'd brought along. She also made one for herself that said *This Certificate entitles Theodora Troutman to become an actress at any time she chooses.*

Did you know that the original owners of our neighbours' house are buried in the basement walls? she asked me.

What? I said. I was taking Logan's advice and trying to listen to the aberrant sounds of the van and figure out a way of describing them.

That's not true, said Logan.

Yeah, it is, said Thebes.

That guy was full of shit, he said. He was just trying to scare you.

Are you talking about that guy who stole your hatchets? I said.

Yeah, he's a tool, said Logan. Nobody's buried in his house.

They bickered about that for a few minutes and then talked about how an arm and a leg had been found in the Red River, and the newspapers had told people to be on the lookout for body parts, like, yeah, we'd see a leg on the way to school and dust it off and bring it right downtown to Police HQ . . . They went on like that for a while, and I put in one of my CDs and then took it out again because it reminded me of Marc.

Then Logan told Thebes he didn't want to talk about that stuff any more. It was bringing him down and so was a lot of other stuff and he needed to think about something positive. Thebes agreed. She decided to pimp our ride with paper hearts and rainbows.

Logan told us about his latest dream. A thousand people were gathered in his school gymnasium and one of his teachers was giving a very mean and sad and negative speech about something and then slowly, as he talked, it became more and more joyous, like just incredibly beautiful and celebratory and Logan said he felt, in this dream, so unbelievably great that he did this amazing vertical and slam dunk and it was the most completely satisfying dream he'd ever had.

He looked at his cast. He banged it against the dash a couple of times. Then he looked at the map and said, Monticello, Blanding, Bluff, Mexican Hat, Tuba City, Flagstaff. He wished he had his knife so he could carve those names into the dash.

Do you use an IUD, Hattie? asked Thebes.

What? I said. Why are you asking me that? Min would have stayed calm and classy and answered honestly and respectfully and then maybe have used the occasion for an informative discussion on birth control.

No, I said. Do you? Stop reading that dictionary.

eleven

IN THE WORLD OF CHILDREN, Min was a genius, she could navigate it in her sleep. She could read book after book to them, sing song after song, soothe them for hours, tenderly and humorously cajole them out of their tantrums, build cities and empires with them in the sandbox for an entire day and answer a million questions in a row without ever losing her cool. She had conceived them, given birth to them and nursed them into life. But out there, in that other world, she was continually crashing into things.

I should give her permission to kill herself, I thought. No, not *permission,* that's the wrong word. I should give her my blessing. No, not even blessing. I don't know what it would be that I'd be giving her, necessarily, by telling her she could do whatever she wanted with her life.

One day this guy came to her door and asked her if she had any money, he said his wife and kids were freezing to death somewhere, and she said oh, you know what, no, I'm so sorry. So the guy asked her if she had money in the bank. Well, yeah, she said. A bit. And then the guy said well, I've got my car here, and I know where there's an ATM, why don't we go there right now and you can get some money out of your account. Well, said Min, yeah, okay. So off they go and Min takes out sixty bucks and gives it to him and he asks her if that's all she has and she says yeah, I'm so sorry, and he takes off, and she walks home alone through the icy streets *still* worrying about the guy's wife and kids. And then she tells Cherkis about this and he tells me and asks me what the hell is wrong with that woman? He didn't say it spitefully or angrily. He said it quietly. He shook his head. He was stumped, genuinely. He wanted to know as badly as I did.

Once, after she'd deep-sixed another one of her art projects early in its infancy, Min decided that what she really needed was religion and she started going to some church in the north end, in some dilapidated neighbourhood off Main Street.

At first it was great but then the pastor of the church told the congregation that they were going to start locking the doors of the church during the Sunday sermon because prostitutes were coming in off the street to warm up in the lobby and kids in the hood were coming in off the street to steal coats from the cloakroom.

Min was enraged. Since when does a church lock its doors, and especially to the community's most vulnerable individuals? The next Sunday she brought a lawn chair and plunked it down by the front door, which she'd propped open with a sign that said All Are Welcome, and then, clipboard in hand, counted the number of prostitutes and street kids and other disenfranchised folks entering the church.

None! Zero. She did this Sunday after Sunday, there was no thieving going on at all, and then, when her good work was finished, she stormed the pulpit in the middle of his sermon, grabbed the mike and presented her findings to the entire assembly and said if this was Christianity she didn't want any part of it, she'd rather sell her ass for crack.

We were making good time now, barrelling through the bodacious curves of southeastern Utah and ignoring all impending signs of trouble with the van. At least I was.

You guys happy? I said.

The kids smiled at me like I was a dog chasing my tail, sweet but stupid, and looked away.

Thebes decided that she and Logan should have Art Class in the van. She would be the teacher and he would be her star pupil. She wanted Logan to attempt, somehow, in whatever medium he chose, to render the majestic beauty of our surroundings.

Logan said he didn't want her to impose her definition of art on him and he'd only play if he could do whatever he wanted to do.

Fine, Thebes said. What do you want to do?

Logan asked her if he could use the mannequin head she'd brought along and she reluctantly agreed. She had been saving it for something big, but fine, okay, he could have it. Logan crawled into the back with Thebes, for better access to her art supplies, and they hunkered down and got to work. It was difficult for Logan to work with the cast on, but Thebes helped him out with the finer details. They were at it for hours, it was a long class. At one point Logan asked me to pull over onto the shoulder so he could do something to the head. I wasn't allowed to look. The final project was going to be a surprise.

By the time he finished, his teacher had fallen fast asleep. Okay, he said, here it is. I pulled over again so I could have a decent look at it.

He handed me a bloody mannequin head.

It's called *This Boy Is Obviously Dying,* he said.

On the neck part of the mannequin he'd drawn little pictures of a sun, a girl, the road, a CD player and a basketball jersey.

There's a written explanation that goes with the piece, he said. He handed me a scrap of paper.

I'm driving, I said. Read it to me.

He began: The goal of this piece was to depict a fictional young victim of typical street violence, attaching a certain level of humanity to a conventional urban casualty. To give it as realistic a feel as possible, I took the head onto the shoulder of a highway somewhere in Utah in the afternoon and beat it with a heavy metal rod for ten minutes. I then painted the head to look as though it was bleeding from all the places where it was damaged or scraped up. The images on the lower neck represent two contrasting influences on the dying kid, one material, violent and destructive, and the other loving, peaceful and uplifting. I see the presence of these two divergent influences as a fundamental conflict within everyone. A conflict this kid lost.

God, um . . . yeah, he did, didn't he? I said.

Logan had also included the materials and resources he used for the project: mannequin head, acrylic paint, ballpoint pen, pencil, metal rod, highway shoulder, glue gun.

Where'd you get a metal rod? I asked him.

Thebes, he said.

I put the boy's head on the dash, facing out towards the road. There was so much blood on it and it looked so real. His hair was covered in it and it was dripping down his face. I didn't want to look at it or touch it or attempt to understand it. Logan didn't ask me what I thought. He seemed pretty pleased with it.

It's great, I said. Kind of dark, but great. I like the explanation.

He told me I didn't have to keep it on the dash if I didn't want to. In fact, he said, we could throw it out or burn it. He was just trying to make Thebes happy.

No, no, I said. I like it up here. It makes an interesting contrast with the hearts and rainbows on the back windows. Think it'll bring us luck?

Logan put in a CD and closed his eyes.

Are you going to sleep? I said.

No answer.

Logan?

Yeah?

Are you—?

No, I'm just thinking, he said.

About what?

He kept his eyes closed while he talked. I don't know how to say it, really, he said.

Say what? I asked.

You know, he said, I kind of know that this whole thing wasn't Min's idea. He opened his eyes and looked at me and then turned around and checked to make sure that Thebes was sleeping. Then he closed them again.

Oh . . . yeah? Well, do you—?

And it's cool, it's fine, he said. I mean really.

Yeah? No, really? But do you—?

I'll go to Twentynine Palms with you, he said, but ultimately? I'm going to do what I want to do. I can take care of myself.

Well, maybe, yeah . . . , I said. But you shouldn't have to, right, that's why—

Okay, yeah, he said. But the thing is, and don't, like,

don't think I'm, you know, mad at you or anything, or hurt, or whatever, but the thing is, you don't . . . like, you don't want us, right? He looked at me and smiled. A genuine, beautiful smile that I think was meant to absolve me of any guilt but instead made me want to kill myself.

No way! I said. That's not true at all! That's completely not true. I just think that Cherkis should probably . . . you know . . . he's your dad. He could take care of . . . It's not like—

Yeah, said Logan, maybe. But does he want to? Do you know that? Is he a total dick? Is he a moron? Is he alive? You know? There are a lot of variables . . .

Yeah, that's true, I said, but there are also a—

And, so, but, said Logan, what I was saying before . . . you know, like the bottom line or whatever . . . you don't want me and Thebes. Why would you? You want to go back to Paris and do your . . . whatever you do, there.

No, that's not the bottom line, Logan, it's—

And can I just ask you something? he said.

Yeah!

Do you actually think Mom would let us go? Because, honestly? I don't think so. She'd never—

He shook his head and his voice cracked.

Do you want to go back? I asked. Because we—

Home? he said.

Yeah, I said.

No.

The van was making mysterious noises again and Logan's CD was skipping.

Houston, we have a problem, he said.

So, what I was doing in Paris, I said, was . . . trying to get away from . . . like, far away from . . . basically . . . my family. Not you guys, not you and Thebes, but—

Mom, said Logan.

Kind of, I said. Yeah. All of that. And everything else. But I missed you guys so—

Yeah, he said. He fiddled around with the CD player and then ran his fingers back and forth over the skeletal arm that Thebes had drawn on his cast and then rested his hand briefly on the dying boy's head. Then he picked up the map and held it close to his face and whispered the names of his favourite sequence of towns. Monticello, Blanding, Bluff, Mexican Hat, Kayenta, Tuba City, Flagstaff.

Twentynine Palms, I said.

Twentynine Palms, yeah, he said.

How's the wrist? I asked.

Meh, he said. I can't feel it.

When I left for Paris, Logan was twelve and Thebes was eight. Cherkis had been AWOL for years and Min was drifting. I was at university but had missed so many classes babysitting Logan and Thebes, while Min was in meetings with the voices in her head, that I decided to drop out entirely and go to the airport and fly away.

I saw Marc for the first time at the Pompidou Centre and I stood next to him while he stared at a black painting and asked him if he had a cigarette. He had a friend who worked there and that friend took us up to the roof of the building and we sat there, smoking, and I looked out at

Paris and I looked at Marc and I thought, with surprising accuracy as it turns out, okay, this will be fine for a while. He asked me my name and I told him it was Aurore, and he said ha ha, no it's not, but if that's what you want me to call you, I will. It was the thing I liked best about him for a long time.

Where're we at, yo? said Thebes.

I glanced at her in the rear-view mirror and flashed her a peace sign. Her face was covered in chalk and ink and she must have slept on one of her poems because there were small letters inscribed backwards on one of her cheeks. We're almost in Mexican Hat, I said.

Cool, cool, she said. Hey, Logan, where's your art? Did you finish?

He pointed at the head on the dash. Thebes went quiet, staring. He passed it to her and she had a closer look.

Dude, she said. She stroked the boy's matted hair and looked deeply into his swollen eyes. She examined the tiny sun, girl, road, CD player and basketball jersey that Logan had drawn on the boy's neck. She read the written explanation. She handed the head back to Logan, who returned it to its place on the dash.

Thebes, I said, are you okay? Why aren't you talking?

I don't know, she said. I think I might be depressed.

Logan and I both whipped our heads around to look at her and the van veered towards the dotted line. Nobody gets away with using the *D* word in our family without a team of trauma experts, a squad of navy SEALs, Green

Berets and a HazMat crew appearing instantaneously in the midst.

Just kidding, said Thebes. Dope art, Lo. There's nothing more I can teach you.

Thanks, T., said Logan. I'll never forget what you've done for me.

El Corazón, said Thebes, and tapped her chest twice with her fist.

We were driving through the Valley of the Gods, getting close to the Arizona border. Cliffs, canyons, mesas and buttes. It was hot, and the light and the shadows were spectacular and shifting and everything looked like it was on fire, red and orange and eroded and ancient and dry. Navajo territory.

Mexican Hat itself was tiny, maybe fifty people, named after a rock formation that looked like an upside-down sombrero. We stopped at a roadside stand and bought some burritos and fruit from a silent family with seventeen kids who kept popping up out of nowhere like spam, and sat on a rock overlooking the valley.

Where are the gods? asked Thebes. Salsa dribbled down her chin and onto her eggshell suit.

I can't watch you eat, said Logan.

Nobody asked you to, said Thebes.

I was hoping we'd make it to Flagstaff, at least, before the van broke down. We had about two hundred miles to go. Troutmans, let's move, I said. I hadn't seen a garage or a gas station for a long time. Thebes dibsed the front seat, Logan sighed heavily, a sigh for the ages, and we all piled back into the mother ship.

And now, said Thebes, for poetry!

Noooooo, said Logan. I'm not playing.

Thebes squinted her eyes and pointed her pistol at Logan. Shit list, she said. It was the first time I'd heard her swear.

Logan put on his headphones. He'd taken off his hoodie in the heat but he pulled his T-shirt up over his face and lay down in the back seat.

Thebes put her feet up on the dash, next to the boy's head, and turned my music down. What do you want to talk about? she asked me.

My first choice was nothing and my second choice was nothing too, there was so much that I needed to think about, but I told her we could talk about whatever she wanted to talk about.

Have you ever had one of those out-of-body experiences? she asked. Like, where you see yourself . . . like getting into a car or on a swing set or something like that? Like, for that split second you really believe that the person you're seeing is actually you?

Yes, I said. I was listening hard, but to the van, trying to determine if it was still making that sound.

That's wild, eh? she said.

Yeah, I said. It *was* making that sound.

When Logan and I were little, she said, we only knew one number: 911.

Well, if you're going to know only one, I guess . . . , I said.

Then she told me a story. One day we were bored, so we called it eight times in a row, she said.

They had hung up every time the operators answered. But eventually the 911 people sent six cruisers to their house with lights flashing and sirens wailing. Min looked out the window and said oh, bite me hard in the ass. She asked the kids what was going on. They told her what they had done. They'll charge us with mischief, said Min. Or neglect. Or some damn thing. (Another thing about our family, apparently, was that we were never able to define, precisely, or understand the charges being brought against us. Patterns of incomprehension.) Min ran to the kitchen, grabbed the cast-iron frying pan from the top of the microwave, plunked it on the floor and messed up her hair. The cops banged on the door and she opened it and told them, in a thick Eastern European accent, that everything was okay now, she was so sorry, she had wanted to heat up some perogies, her frying pan had fallen on her head, she had been knocked out for a minute or two, her husband was at work, her children had panicked but were self-conscious about their English and afraid to speak to the 911 operator. No, she had not been assaulted. No, they had not been broken into. She told them she loved Canada. She told them she loved horses. Thebes didn't know why she'd said that. The cops asked the kids if they were okay. They said yeah. The cops told the kids that next time there was an emergency at home they should attempt to speak with the 911 operators, even though their English wasn't good. They said okay. The cops left and Logan and Thebes watched them laugh all the way back to their cars.

Hmm, I said. I smiled at Thebes. Your old lady rules. So I guess you've stopped calling 911?

It was one of those stories that could have gone in so many different directions. Had Thebes been embarrassed when she saw the cops laughing? Stricken with the realization that the cops knew her mom was nuts, hadn't believed a word she'd said, and thought it was hilarious? Or had she been proud of Min's wacky resourcefulness, sure that the cops had bought it, or, even if they hadn't bought it, had been impressed with the effort, and had gone away feeling happy. Another trippy day of serving and protecting. Was Thebes trying to tell me that Min could handle tricky situations if she needed to, that all was not lost, that she could live life on life's terms, or was she trying to tell me that Min had seemed crazy to her for a long time?

I think we're in Arizona, said Thebes. I liked the way she sat up in her seat then and looked around with fresh eyes, like things might be radically different now that we had crossed an invisible state line.

twelve

I WAS AT MIN'S PLACE when Cherkis left. I played with Logan in the backyard while Min, with baby Thebes on her hip, chased Cherkis down the front sidewalk, screaming obscenities and at the same time begging him not to go. A few of the neighbours had come out to watch.

Logan was wearing a red plastic fireman's hat and was pretending to put out a fire with the garden hose. I was a burn victim and wasn't allowed to move. Every time I heard Min shriek I'd turn my head and try to get up, but Logan would race over to me, put his hands on my cheeks and his face close to mine and attempt to redirect my focus. You'll be okay, he said. Don't worry. You're gonna make it. You won't die. And then he'd race back to the fire.

Later on, after Cherkis had successfully managed to escape, Min lay sobbing on the living room floor and Logan sat beside her watching TV. I tried to get him to come for a walk with me and Thebes but he said no, he wanted to watch the Ninja Turtles with Min. When we got back I told Min that I was going to leave for a few hours but that I'd be back that evening to make dinner and help her get the kids to bed and after that I'd hang out with her and sleep over if she wanted me to. I tried to talk to her about Cherkis, about everything, but there was nothing she wanted to say or hear.

It took me forever to leave because Logan had hidden my shoes and wouldn't tell me where.

Thebes convinced Logan to play Deborah Solomon's Q and A.

Okay, she said, I'm Deborah Solomon and you are you. Logan Troutman, she said. You've experienced a lot of failure in the past. What makes you think this venture will be a success?

Logan: What do you mean *failure*? Fuck off.

Thebes, interjecting as herself, told Logan that he

wouldn't really say that to Deborah Solomon. Remember, it's *The New York Times,* she said. Let me start again.

Logan Troutman, she said. You've experienced a lot of failure in the past. What makes you think this venture will be a success?

Logan: What venture?

Okay, cut, said Thebes. Logan, please work with me here.

It's not TV, he said, it's print. It's a column. You don't say "cut." God.

Okay, said Thebes. The venture I'm talking about is this trip to find Cherkis. Okay?

Deborah Solomon doesn't get all personal in her columns, said Logan.

Well, this time she is, okay? said Thebes. I'm going to start again.

Logan Troutman, she said. You've experienced a lot of failure in the past. What makes you think this venture will be a success?

Logan: I have a very positive mental attitude. Plus, it helps that I really don't care.

Solomon: Well, which one is it? A positive mental attitude or you just don't care?

Logan: I just don't care.

He said he was done with the game and was going to lie down.

Any of those secrets you'd like to cash in on? Thebes said to me.

What are you talking about? I said.

Your certificate, she said.

Oh yeah! I said. Okay. Yes. You are the coolest, most beautiful kid on the planet. You're my inspiration and my rock and the wind beneath my sails. You are the shit, T.T.

That's not a secret, she said. And don't be sarcastic. Tell me something about yourself that you haven't told anybody.

I thought for a long time.

Okay, I said. I had sex with my swimming coach when I was sixteen and he was thirty-seven and then I blackmailed him and told him I was pregnant and needed five hundred dollars for an abortion or I'd tell his wife that he was a pervert and he gave me the money and I spent it all on acid and mushrooms and quit the swim team.

Thebes silently reached around to the back seat, dug out her hole puncher, took my certificate out of the glove compartment and ceremoniously punched a hole in the first box.

You can't tell anybody, I said.

Ew, she said. As if. Besides, this seals it. She waved the certificate around.

I worried that I had chosen the wrong secret to share with an eleven-year-old. I apologized to her for being indiscreet.

Well, Hattie, she said, I'm on shaky ground here. It's not my department. Just remember that not all your secrets have to be disgusting, all right? Like, were you a slut when you were young?

No! I said. I wanted to mention that I'd been lonely, vulnerable, pathetically enamoured with this guy's twisted attention, probably conducting a misguided search for a father figure, periodically terrified of my sister, whom I loved and revered but never understood, definitely insecure about my body and my brain, wanting to be adored by somebody adorable, lousy at swimming, on the verge of an eating disorder and dangerously impulsive . . . but that would have dragged this thing out even further.

She let it go. She asked me if I remembered how Grandma used to brag about her ability to memorize fifty three-letter words a day.

I saw a gas station down the road and decided to stop and fill up. Thebes could buy a *Tiger Beat* or something and focus on teenage mishaps other than mine and we could drive in silence for a while, maybe. Logan was sprawled out in the back seat, asleep and oblivious to the bass that was still pumping out of his headphones loud enough that the guy filling the van with gas started nodding his head in time with the beat and said he loved that band.

I told Thebes to go check out the magazines and then darted around to the side of the gas station to use the pay phone. There was no answer at the hospital. Had it been evacuated? Firebombed? Were the inmates rioting, throwing mattresses out the windows and cutting off the phone lines? When doesn't a hospital answer its phone?

I went back to the van and talked to the gas jockey.

That's a kick-ass mohawk, I said. Can I . . . ?

Sure, he said, and leaned over so I could graze it with my fingertips. You know you're leaking oil, he said. Big time.

I know, I said, what do I do about it?

Well, you fix it, he said. It took him half an hour to get those four words out. I smiled.

Dude, *how* do I fix it? I said. He told me if it was a wonky seal or a busted gasket it would cost a lot, maybe five hundred bucks, and would take probably an entire day to fix. An oil leak is not good, he concluded, half a century later.

Do you think I can make it to Flagstaff? I said.

Yabsolutely, he said. He asked if he could come along. He had a girlfriend there whose head he wanted to break. I told him I wasn't going to give him a ride if what he had in mind was domestic violence and he said no, no, he was only kidding. He just wanted to talk to her about her bad habits.

What about your job? I asked him.

I'm quitting right now, this second, he said.

Thebes came hopping over on one foot with an Archie comic and a new knife for Logan. She laid it across his throat for him to find if he ever woke up.

We got into the van and I started it up while he and Thebes were chatting. Logan slept through all of this. The guy's name was Colt.

Colt, said Thebes. Like a baby, male horse?

I guess, said the guy, or a gun.

Well, which do you prefer? she said.

What do you mean? he asked.

Like, how do you prefer to think of yourself? As a baby, male horse?

No, he said, he didn't really like to think of himself that way.

Well, then, as a gun? she said.

No, not really, he said. He preferred basically not to think of himself at all.

Isn't that impossible? she said. How can you not think of yourself at all?

Well, he said, he just thought about other things.

Such as? said Thebes.

About his girlfriend, mostly, he said.

Yeah, she said, but not in relation to yourself? He didn't think so. Anything else? said Thebes.

Well, I do think about life on other planets, he said.

Really? she said.

He said yeah, he thought a lot about this planet called Moralia.

C'mon, she said, there is no planet called Moralia.

This was good. I'd picked up a violent nutcase named after a gun who believed in a planet that didn't exist.

Do you mind if I smoke? he asked.

Not at all . . . may I have one of those? I said.

Actually, we do mind, said Thebes.

Then she started relating to this guy by telling him how, when she was a little kid, she had this magazine and in it was an advertisement for this miniature fake town called Thomas Kinkade Lamplight Village. She wanted to live there so badly. She would lie in her bed gazing at this village, with its cute gabled houses and meandering, narrow pathways and smoking chimneys and thatched roofs and homey lanterns and warm, orange glow and cry her eyes out wishing she was in it.

Word, said Colt, I'm down. I wished I lived on Moralia. Thebes had found a soulmate in this homicidal cosmonaut. Impeccably, sombrely united in their mutual, impossible longing to live in places that weren't real, they high-fived and punched and slapped and then gazed for a while out the window at the real world, the one they'd had it with.

Nice head, said Colt, finally. He pointed to the dash.

Yeah, I said. The guy sleeping next to you with the knife on his throat made it in Thebes's art class.

Who's Thebes? he said.

That one, I said, nodding my head in Thebes's direction.

In Old English, said Thebes, *colt* means young ass or camel. She slammed her dictionary shut.

Hey, isn't the Grand Canyon around here somewhere? she said.

Hey, another chunk of the world missing from our lives. Another giant hole in the surface of our universe. Let's find it!

Yabsolutely, said Colt. Where are you guys from, anyway?

The True North strong and free, said Thebes.

Cool, he said, where are you going?

Twentynine Palms, she said.

Where's that? he asked.

California, she said.

What for?

To meet our father, she said.

Are you the mother? he asked me.

I'm the aunt, I said.

Then Colt told us a story about how he was a conduit for love, but I'd stopped listening.

Logan woke up and he and Colt politely introduced themselves to each other and then Thebes said we had to see the Grand Canyon. I said I was worried about the van and really wanted to get to Flagstaff. But Logan said yeah, he wouldn't mind checking out the canyon, and Colt said he wouldn't mind either, he had a window before he was scheduled to break his girlfriend's head.

I don't know what to say about the Grand Canyon that the name itself doesn't evoke. It's big and deep and brown. The four of us stood at the edge of it and looked down and saw a line of donkeys with tourists on them snaking along a path at the bottom.

With her underwater camera Thebes took a picture of Logan, Colt and me beside the canyon looking slightly dazed and disappointed.

Let's get outta here, I said. It gave me the creeps. I snapped at Thebes to back away from the edge. I yelled at Logan when he pretended to push her over, *that's so not fucking funny,* and begged Colt for one of his smokes. *Yabsolutely!*

I glared at a swarm of tourists who were staring like they recognized me from *Rosemary's Baby* and flicked my butt into the canyon when I was done.

Logan wanted to drive into Flagstaff, so I let him, partly in a glasnost attempt to make up for screaming at him earlier. Wild West. And mostly he was using one hand, his good one, to drive. Someday he'd have a valid licence and in the meantime he needed to practise. I knew he thought it looked lame to be riding into a new town with his sister and his aunt and I knew he thought Colt was a goof. Ideally he would have had us all duck down and make ourselves invisible while he drove around listening to his tunes, playing it cool, pretending he was something other than a fifteen-year-old Canadian boy in a leaking Ford Aerostar minivan.

We dropped Colt off in a 7-Eleven parking lot. He said he needed to buy a newspaper and a razor and some other things and he could get to where he was going from there.

Not Moralia, said Thebes. Later, skater. She was yawning.

Hey, I said, act nice and gentle, eh? Nice meeting you.

You too, said Colt. Thanks for the ride.

Take it easy, said Logan. They shook hands, awkwardly because of his cast.

Logan peeled out of the parking lot and we drove around looking for a hotel. It was late, around ten, and I'd have to find a garage in the morning. We found a cheap Motel 6 and while I checked us in and Thebes lay down on a ratty sofa in the lobby and read some literature on Flagstaff, Logan carried our stuff to the room. When Thebes and I got there the TV was blaring and Logan was pacing around, fuming.

That fucker jacked my knife, he said.

Colt? said Thebes. The new one I bought you?

Yeah, he said, when I was sleeping. He must have.

I lay on the bed and closed my eyes. We'll buy you a new one, I said. We'll just keep buying knives and pistols.

Thebes lay down beside me and continued to read her brochures. Did you know that Flagstaff has a disproportionate number of methamphetamine addicts and scam artists? she said.

I didn't know why a hotel would have a brochure with that kind of information. Is there anything in there about horseback riding or museums or anything like that? I asked. I thought maybe there'd be something fun to do the next day while the van was getting fixed.

Um, said Thebes, it says there's a psychiatric museum housed in an abandoned mental asylum somewhere around here. Apparently it's haunted with—

Okay, no, we're not doing that. Maybe we'll see a movie or something.

Logan asked if he could take the van and drive around and look for a basketball court.

No, I said. I was an ugly wall of no. It's late. It's dark. And I don't trust the van. And didn't you hear what Thebes just said? This place is crawling with meth-heads. I was also afraid that he'd try to find Colt to get his knife back, but I didn't want to tell him that in case he hadn't actually thought of it.

And can you turn that TV off? I said.

He went into the bathroom and slammed the door and turned on the shower.

I lay on the bed with my eyes closed and tried to calm myself down doing some yogic breathing Marc had tried to teach me as an alternative to Gauloises. Thebes was quiet too. She was tired. She was already under the blanket. Her holster and the tourist brochures lay on the floor beside the bed.

Thebie? I said.

Yo.

Tomorrow you should have a bath. And brush your hair.

Why? she said.

Tomorrow we get to Twentynine Palms, I said. I can help you with your hair if you want.

Tomorrow?

Yeah, I'm pretty sure we'll be there tomorrow. Tomorrow night. If we can get the van fixed in the morning, I said.

I was waiting for her to talk, to spring into action, to illuminate the room with some Theban fact or question or comment or pronouncement or definition or something, anything. I stroked her hair. I put my arms around her and held her close and she didn't say a word. I wouldn't think about it. I wouldn't think about the possibility of this being our last night together for a long time. I could hear Logan swearing in the shower. I could hear Marc breathing next to me. I could hear my father cracking a lame joke and I could hear Min laughing.

thirteen

I WOKE UP AROUND MIDNIGHT and tried as delicately
as I could to extricate myself from Thebes's Jurassic grip
and to get out of bed and find a cigarette in my backpack.
I was trying, and failing, for the most part, to smoke only
while she was unconscious. And then I noticed that Logan
wasn't in the other bed. And he wasn't in the bathroom.
And he wasn't in the closet. He wasn't in our motel room,

period. I went to the window and moved the curtain and looked outside at the parking lot.

Yeah, the van was gone. Of course it was.

I know the score, boy, I thought to myself. I've run away too. I sat on the edge of the tub in the dark with the fan on and finished my cigarette and then wrote a note for Thebes in case she woke up and wondered why she was all alone.

I wandered down the road and passed a bunch of other cheap motels and cheesy chain restaurants and closed gas stations. If there had been a church I'd have gone inside and prayed. I would have said *please bring the little fucker back safe and sound, God, I mean it*. But instead the most I could do was say his name over and over. Logan, I whispered. Logan, Logan, Logan. Where the hell are you? I passed a panhandler sitting under a streetlight at an intersection and he had a sign that said Need 37 Million Dollars for Trip to Space. I could get behind that. I gave him two bucks. I headed for a bar across the street and ducked inside to find the pay phone, punched my old Paris number and listened to it ring and ring and ring.

When I went back out to the parking lot some hippies looked up at me from their toke and said hey.

What's up? I said.

Check out the moon, man, said one of them. He pointed up like maybe I was one of those people who always forgot things like keys and wallets and the location of the moon.

I stared at it for what seemed like a really long time. I didn't see Logan in any of the moon's craters or shadows.

It's really beautiful, I said. And I mean really beautiful. Seriously.

The stoners nodded and agreed and asked me if I wanted to join them.

Thanks, I said. But I can't. I'm looking for someone.

Who are you looking for? one of them asked.

My nephew, I said. His name is Logan. He's fifteen. This tall. Black hoodie. He's driving a Ford Aerostar.

Whoa! said the guy. Wait. Who?

My nephew, I said.

Man, he said, how'd you lose him?

We're staying at a motel down there and I fell asleep and he took off, I said.

That's messed up, he said.

Yeah.

Think you'll find him? he said.

What do you mean? I asked. Like, ever? Yeah. He's probably off shooting somewhere.

What? said the guy.

Hoops, I said. Basketball.

It's like the middle of the night, he said.

Hey, do you guys have a car? I asked.

Noooooo, said the guy. Nope.

Yeah we do, Ding Dong, said a girl from the huddle.

We do? said the guy.

It's a truck, said a different guy. He had his arm around the girl.

The car is a truck? said the guy. Cool.

Do you guys want to drive around and help me look for him? I said.

Oh, yeah! They were into that.

I sat in the box with a few of them, including Ding Dong, who said it was totally dope with him if I sat in his lap, and the girl drove. We watched one another's hair go wild in the wind and the clouds cover and uncover the moon like a blanket, like a nervous mother. It would have been a great time if I hadn't just lost my sister's kid.

None of the people in the truck were actually from Flagstaff, they were all seasonal employees from somewhere else, so they didn't really know where the basketball courts might be.

Before we could begin our search we had to go to one of their dorms or lodges or whatever and pick up some more weed. I asked Ding Dong if it was close and he said yeah and that Ding Dong wasn't actually his name, it was Adam.

When we got there the others got out of the truck and went in, but Adam said they'd be fine, they could get the stuff, why didn't he and I just sit there and talk.

I told him I liked the idea of talking but I was pre-occupied with my missing nephew and didn't really know what to say. I wanted to find Logan. Adam said we'd find Logan. He knew it. He told me a lot of things about himself. He and a friend of his had just been fired by a Spanish religious radio station called Radio Sinai for translating Cheech and Chong dialogues into Spanish and airing them late at night. Or something like that. I found out that he wasn't close to his father at all but that he and his mother talked pretty often, even though she wasn't really in touch with her own emotions. He had a girlfriend, sort of, whom he'd recently reconnected with after a couple of years of not talking. She was an actress and sweet but they screamed at each other a lot. He didn't think she really appreciated him. His sister was a single mother with an eight-year-old daughter and they hung out. He helped her when he could. He told me he spoke a little Sango, a dialect of Ngbandi. He asked me what my nephew and I were doing in Flagstaff and I told him the whole story. When I had finished he put his hand on mine and said he was sorry I was so unhappy. He asked me if I thought all this stuff was happening for a reason.

No, I said. I don't think so. Where do you think the others are? I asked him.

Then he asked me if I'd heard of the Heisenberg Uncertainty Principle.

I'm not sure, I said.

He told me it was the idea that the momentum and location of a certain particle cannot be determined at the same time.

Wow, that's pretty interesting, I said. I told him I was going to walk back to the hotel because all of this was taking too long and I had to check on Thebes.

No, man, hold up, he said. I'll go find out what the deal is. I'll be right back. Please don't go, he said. Okay? Please?

I stared some more at the moon and at the rippled surface of the box that I was sitting in. I thought about how good it felt to have somebody ask me to stay. I thought about how pathetic it was that it felt so good to have some-body ask me to stay. Adam came running back to the truck and said that the others were so done, they'd kind of for-gotten about us, they were gonna hang out at the lodge and watch *Drugstore Cowboy* but they'd given him the key to the truck. They'd said to wish me luck with the search.

Let's blast, he said.

We drove back to the motel first so I could peek in on Thebes. I told Adam he could wait in the truck but he said he'd like to come with me. We went to the room and stood in the doorway and looked at the sleeping Thebes.

I like her hair, Adam whispered. I nodded and smiled. You're a good aunt, he said.

I shook my head and whispered no, I wasn't. I was a disaster. He put his arm around my shoulder and we looked at Thebes for another minute or two, like we were the brand-new parents of an oversized baby girl, and then we quietly left the room and went back to the truck.

He asked me if I had a boyfriend and I said yeah, well, no, past tense. But I still loved him. I thought I did.

Adam said that was cool, that was beautiful, right, why should I stop, we were always meant to be moving in a love direction, always.

We drove around the dark suburban streets of Flagstaff looking for basketball courts and Logan. Adam played an old Pavement CD and talked the whole time about a variety of things and I tried to listen and occasionally interject with some thought of my own or some polite encouragement but mostly I was thinking about what a colossal mess I'd made of things and trying mentally to defibrillate myself. I was seeing Logan everywhere and then not seeing him. I was having a panic attack. I was having trouble breathing. Adam stopped talking and put his hand on my knee and asked me if I was okay.

No, I said.

Do you want to stop for a minute? he asked.

No, I said.

Different music? he said.

No, no, it's good, I said.

We'll find him, said Adam, I guarantee it. Honestly. We won't stop looking until we do.

I told Adam about my father, how he'd drowned in the ocean after rescuing Min and me. And how I used to search for Min all the time when we were kids. She'd take off and scare the shit out of everyone, I said. One time she broke out of the hospital and ran eight miles in a rainstorm in her nightgown, barefoot, with cops chasing her the whole time.

I told Adam how I was still hoping to be with Marc someday, how futile *that* was, and how tomorrow was the day that we were supposed to find Cherkis, but probably wouldn't. I told him that Min had run away, again, from the psych ward and that Logan had said he was going to do whatever he wanted to do and I didn't know what any of it meant.

Adam parked the truck in front of some ugly, prefab houses and turned off the ignition. He looked around at the houses and drummed his fingers against the steering wheel.

Canadians are not that different from us, after all, he said. What would happen if you slid over just a little?

Well, we'd be closer, I said. I slid over and he put his arm around my shoulders, again, and sang a Leon Redbone song in a really low key.

My mom used to sing that to me, he said.

I thanked him for his friendship and he said I was welcome and thanked me for mine and then he started the truck again, I slid back to my side, and we resumed our search for Logan.

We finally found him at a court next to a high school, not too far from the motel. It was pitch black but he'd aimed the van lights at one of the hoops so he could see what he was doing. He was playing music softly too, some soul. When we saw him I asked Adam to stop the truck so we could watch him shoot for a few minutes and I could cry from monumental relief without him noticing.

I told you we'd find him, said Adam.

C'mon, I said, we both know you didn't have a clue.

Mmm, yeah, but you gotta bel—

Don't say you gotta believe, I said.

Nope, okay, he said, I wasn't. I was gonna say *you gotta bleed.*

We were quiet, watching Logan make basket after basket and trying to hear what music he had playing in the van, but it wasn't loud enough.

So, Hattie, he said.

So, Adam, I said.

Would you be at all interested in necking for a short, short period of time, he said. I mean, look, he pointed at Logan, the kid's all right, right? Although he does have a cast.

I said no, I didn't want to neck, I had to assemble the troops, reunite the troika, but I'd like to kiss him at least once.

Have you ever kissed an American? he asked.

Hmmmm, I said, let me think about that for a minute. He waited. No, I said, not really, no. Have you ever kissed a Canadian?

Well, yeah, he had, you know how it goes. He smiled and shrugged.

Yeah, no, I said. I kissed him.

Goodbye, Adam.

Goodbye, Hattie.

Love direction, he said.

I said, Always, dude, 'til the end of time, and got out of the truck and walked towards the light.

Logan was wearing shiny, black basketball shorts way down low on his hips, with blood red boxers bubbling up on top, like he'd cut a major artery in his ass. He'd taken his T-shirt and hoodie off and his back was shiny with sweat. He was skinny and pale. Scars, faded hickeys and plaster cast. Where had he got that scar from anyway? He was darting around under the net, blocking and being blocked by imaginary players and going in for layup after layup.

Hey, gangster, I said, your pants are falling off.

He whirled around and then back again, to the net, and caught his rebound and stood there breathing heavily and looking at me.

What are you doing here? he asked me.

Give me that, I said. He threw me his ball and I took a few shots and missed.

Okay, I said, quick game of Horse, let's hurry, Thebes is alone in the room.

I thought you'd be really mad, said Logan. It had started to rain and Marvin Gaye was singing "What's Going On" softly in the van.

I am really mad, I said, but I don't know what to do about it.

He beat me at Horse and then as we walked to the van we took turns throwing the ball, hard, at each other. I aimed for his head but he caught it every time and beaned it back at mine.

Jerk, I said.

Control freak, he said.

What? I said. You have *got* to be kidding me.

Not really, he said, you're—

I'm gonna break your other arm, I said.

We got into the van and it wouldn't start and I hit the steering wheel with the heel of my hand the way my father used to do when his car, along with all the other aspects of his life, broke down.

Oh, for fuck's sake, I said, now you've killed the battery. I tried again.

Well, don't flood it, man, said Logan.

I thought about the other options I'd had that evening, the roads less travelled. I could have been necking with a sweet, American hippie in the back of a truck under a full yellow moon. At the very least I could have been asleep with Thebes, the human giraffe, all tangled up around me. Or, maybe, I could have been in Paris singing like Piaf and swinging from street lamps with a bottle of Bordeaux in one hand and Marc at an open window with a flower box, beckoning me to join him upstairs for some gallant lovemaking and some shrugging off of life's tiresome little tragedies.

How did you find me? asked Logan.

By looking, I said.

I'm just asking, he said, you don't have to—

Just . . . you know what? I said. I shook my head. Let's not talk. Let's pray.

I don't pray, he said.

Do now, I said. Pray that this fucking piece of shit will start so we can get the hell out of here.

We were quiet for a minute. Our eyes were closed. Okay, I said. Here we go. I tried to start the van and nothing happened.

We gave up on prayer and got out of the van and played another game of Horse and then tried the van again. This time it started, and we took off for the motel.

Somehow I'd lost my room key, maybe I'd left it in Adam's truck, and Logan hadn't bothered to take one when he left, so I had to go to the front desk and ask for another one. The woman asked me if I had a little girl with me.

Well, yeah, I said, she's in the room.

She's been making some long-distance phone calls

all the way up to Canada, said the woman. I had to help her with the code.

Thanks, I said. I'm really sorry—

I thought about calling the police, said the woman.

What? I said. Why?

She was all alone, said the woman. How was I supposed to know you hadn't left her there?

Yeah, well, yeah, but . . . I know, but she was okay, right? I had to go find this guy—I pointed at Logan—and I did check on her at one point . . . I know. I know. Normally . . . I left her a note, I added.

The woman turned around and started fiddling with the fax machine. The sun was coming up.

All right, I said. Can I just . . . okay, thank you, really, thank you for not calling the cops. I appreciate it.

Checkout's at eleven, she said.

Thebes was sitting on the edge of the bed. She'd changed out of her dirty white suit and back to her old royal blue terry cloth outfit. She was looking at the TV but it wasn't on. Her hands were folded in her lap and she didn't say anything when we came in.

Thebie, I said. I sat down beside her and put my arms around her. I'm so sorry. Are you okay? You got my note, right? Are you hungry?

Logan came over and put his hand up for five but she didn't lift hers. Thebes? he said. She began to cry. Logan sat down on the bed and said he felt so bad, this was all his fault, he would let her sit in the front of the van and do

poetry with her if she wanted him to. Or crafts, or whatever. She could have permanent control of the remote.

I took her hands in mine and saw thin red scratch
marks on the inside of her wrists. Thebie, I whispered. I
kissed her hands. Thebie, I said again.

Logan hadn't noticed. He got up and said he was
going to have a shower and went into the bathroom. Then
he came back out.

Thebes! Dude! he said. You found my knife! Thanks!
He went back into the bathroom.

Thebes, I said. What did you do? She didn't say anything. Please, Thebie, talk to me, I said. Tell me what
happened, okay? I won't tell anyone, I promise. Not even
Logan. I won't tell a soul.

She told me she had woken up and we were gone and
she was afraid and worried. She had noticed that the van
was gone too. She hadn't seen the note until later. She
didn't know what to do at first. Then she decided to call
the hospital to see if she could talk to Min. She phoned
the front desk to ask for help, and eventually, after six or
seven tries, managed to get through to the hospital. The
nurse told her it was the middle of the night and Thebes
said she was sorry to be calling so late but Min was her
mom and she really needed to talk to her. Somehow, for
some reason, the nurse had said all right, she'd see if she
could wake Min up. Then a few minutes later Min was on
the phone. She said hello. Thebes was so excited she was
jumping from bed to bed. Min! she said. It's me! At that
point in the story Thebes started crying again. Logan
came out of the washroom.

What's up? he said. What's wrong?

I told him I needed to talk to Thebes, alone, and asked him to go back into the washroom. He said no problem and left.

What did she say? I asked Thebes. She was crying too hard to answer. I bet she was so happy to hear your voice, I said. I held her some more and let her cry. What did she say? I asked her again. Finally, Thebes had stopped crying long enough to speak.

She kept calling me Hattie, she said. She thought I was you.

She did? I said.

And every time I'd say no, no, Min, this is Thebes, it's Thebie. Theodora. Remember? But she didn't know who I was and she just kept calling me Hattie and asking me if I had the tickets for some show she wanted to see and I didn't know what to say. I kept saying this is Thebes, this is Thebes. And then she'd say like, oh, Hattie, what are we going to wear or stuff like that and then finally I just said no, I didn't have the tickets but I'd get them and I'd call her back. And that was it.

Oh god, Thebes, I said. She's on so much medication, you know? And she'd probably been fast asleep, like in the middle of a dream or something of when she was young, and probably right after she hung up she thought to herself, wait, hold on! That was Thebes! Not Hattie! But she couldn't call you back because she didn't know where you were calling from and probably the nurse made her go back to bed, and tomorrow when we call her it'll all be clear and we'll just . . . laugh, right?

Thebes didn't think anybody was going to be laughing. No, she said, well, maybe. Well, no. She said she guessed she should have that bath I'd been talking about before. Wash her hair, all that.

Logan came out of the washroom and I asked him for just two more minutes alone with Thebes. Yep, he said, and turned around again.

So, then, after you talked to Min . . . you did this? I said. I touched her wrists. She said yeah, but she wasn't serious. She was just fooling around and bored and didn't know what else to do. She hadn't meant it. I thought of all the times Thebes had pretended to be somebody else on the phone and now when she was being herself it hadn't worked out.

Hey, come over here, I said, and led her by the hand to the window. See, I said, look at that. I pointed to the sun the way Adam had earlier directed me to the moon. Over there, I said. I didn't know what to say but I kept talking. It's coming up, I said. It's shining like a champ. I didn't know what to do besides pointing out something that was constant in her life, even if it was only an uninhabitable ball of fire that you couldn't look at without flinching or experiencing pain.

Yeah, so? said Thebes.

Yeah, I said, you see? *See what? What was I trying to accomplish?* I told Thebes about how when Min and I were kids we got to see a solar eclipse and the whole world went dark. We wore welding helmets, I said. Min got them from some body shop guys she knew. We were out in a field with these giant black things on our heads, they covered our faces, we looked like Darth Vader, we were laughing, Min was standing there all, *Luke, I am your father,* you know, and waiting for it to happen, it only happens once, maybe twice, in a person's lifetime. Min was super-excited about it but I hadn't really cared. Oh, the sun gets obliterated, day turns to night, big whoop, but she forced me out there, she came to my school and dragged me out of class, and we lay on our backs in this field and watched the whole thing, it was so wild, it was amazing, and Min told me that she loved the sun, that if the sun was ever permanently erased she wouldn't know what to do, but as long as the sun was around, you know, she was okay, and the thing about the eclipse for her was not about the sun being covered up and the uniqueness of that but about it coming back. You know? So . . . there it is, again, you know?

Sure, said Thebes. She patted my knee.

Think it'll rain? I asked her.

Why should it? she said.

I understood what my mother had gone through with Min. How she'd tried so hard to come up with something, anything, to jar Min's thinking, to get her to laugh or to hope or to live.

It's an illness, she told me one afternoon in the car, it's not rational. I don't know what to say to her any more. Sometimes I pray that God will take her, that she'll die, and this will all be over.

I hadn't known what to say to that. If I'd had a knife at the time I'd probably have been carving random thoughts into the dash too, like Logan.

Later that evening she apologized for scaring me. She told me she didn't really want to kill herself, she was just so tired and desperate and afraid of losing Min and of not understanding what it was she was supposed to be doing to help her.

Help me to die.

No, never.

I thought of those cheesy *Love is* . . . cartoons. Love is . . . killing your sister when she asks you to? Love is . . . refusing to kill your sister when she asks you to? I had trouble deciding between leaded and unleaded at the gas station and skim or 2% at the 7-Eleven, how was I supposed to choose the definition of my love for Min?

One day I came home from school and found Min taping up the windows of the car in the garage. I asked her why she'd waited until four in the afternoon, when she *knew* I'd be coming home, to tape up the windows. She told me it had taken her some time to get going that morning and she started laughing and I got really mad and shoved her against the car and told her I wished she was a dog because dogs don't kill themselves and she said she wished she was a dog too, and then she started to cry and I told her I was sorry for shoving her against the car and she went in and I peeled off all the tape from the windows and made a big ball out of it and threw it on the roof of the house. When I went inside, she handed me two bullets. Here, she said, take these too. I asked her why she had bullets, did she have a gun, and she said no, she didn't have a gun. I went outside and threw the bullets on the roof and then went back in and watched TV with Min for a few hours until dinner. Min tried to say a few things to me but every time she started to talk I'd put my hand up and say, I've had enough of this bullshit. I should have listened to every word she had to say but I was so freaked out that even the stupid, predictable words coming from the TV didn't make any sense to me.

Thebes, I said, do you want to have a pillow fight?

Do you?

Well, I don't know, it could be fun . . . do you?

I guess, if you do.

So for the next half-hour or so, while the Dickwad family in the room next to us pounded on their walls and told us to shut up, I fought the kids with a Polyfil pillow and eventually let them beat me into a fetal position on the floor. It was maybe seven-thirty or eight in the morning. I had to get the van into a shop, but this time we were all going together.

First, though, Thebes had a long, hot bath and I washed her hair and tried to dig the chunks of dirt out of her scalp without removing her brains. How long before this dye comes out? I asked her.

I don't know, she said. Ten or twelve washes.

Well, shit, I said, you'll be like twenty-two years old before it's gone.

Your mama, she said.

No, yours, I said and she splashed water in my face.

fourteen

WE WERE PACKED UP, READY TO GO, Thebes was
clean and shiny, in her secondary white outfit, and Logan
was making a Herculean effort to be charming in spite of
having had no sleep that night and no access to the
remote control. There was a knock at the door. I thought
it would be the cops, the front desk woman with a registered complaint, or the people in the next room waving

nunchuks and cans of mace, but then I remembered that this was the United States and all that would happen was that we'd get our faces blown off and die instantly.

See who it is, Lo, I said. He peered through the peephole and said it was some dude in a toque and he was carrying a ton of stuff.

Like, weapons? I said.

No, said Logan, like casseroles.

It was Adam. I was so happy to see him. I was inordinately happy to see him. I threw my arms around him and all the stuff he had and hauled him into the room and introduced him to Logan and Thebes, who were looking slightly perplexed. I told them how I knew Adam and Adam told them that he'd seen both of them last night without them seeing him.

You're a pretty shooter, he told Logan, who mumbled something, and then Adam told Thebes her hair was awesome and she smiled shyly and thanked him for noticing. She showed him a few of her kung fu moves and he taught her one he knew.

He'd made the casseroles himself as soon as he had dropped me off at the court, and he also brought some CDs he'd burned and a bag of weed. I tossed the bag into my backpack before Logan could see it and thanked Adam for everything and then I tried to lift him off the ground, which was stupid, and told him we were about to check out and find a mechanic and then hit the road to Twentynine Palms. He said he knew of a guy who could fix our van for really cheap, and so we followed him in his truck to this guy's place way out on one edge of Flagstaff.

When we were driving Thebes asked if Adam was a methamphetamine addict or a scam artist and I said no, I didn't think he was either of those things, and he wasn't actually from Flagstaff. And he's not a ghost either, I said.

I almost drove off the road in an effort to keep up with Adam and to surreptitiously observe Thebes in her post-trauma recovery. I didn't know if it was true that she hadn't really meant to hurt herself. Maybe she hadn't really meant to *kill* herself. I didn't know if this was a typical thing for an eleven-year-old to do when her mother couldn't remember who she was and she was on her way to visit a father who also probably couldn't remember who she was.

I'm gonna see if I can use this mechanic's phone and I'll call Min again, I told her.

I wanna talk to her too, said Logan.

Yeah, of course, I said. Then it occurred to me that maybe I had just made a tactical error. I'd assumed that Min would be more coherent on the phone during the day, when she wasn't under the soporific influence of the blue torpedoes, but maybe she'd be just as spaced as before and this time not only would she not know Thebes, she wouldn't know Logan, or me, for that matter, and we'd all want to open up a vein.

I followed Adam onto a gravel driveway and into a yard cluttered with the decaying body parts of old cars, trucks and tractors.

Doesn't look like he's got much of a track record of fixing things, said Logan. A pit bull came flying out of nowhere, barking, and hurled herself against the side of Adam's truck. Holy shit, man, said Logan, I don't do pit bulls. Don't open your door. Thebes said she wasn't afraid and put her hand on the door handle and Logan grabbed it and said, No, Thebie, don't, those dogs are *banned* in Canada.

Give it some of the casserole, I told Thebes. Logan, let her go, you can stay in the van if you want. Hell yeah, he would, thanks, he said. He put his headphones on and dropped out of view.

Adam had got out of his truck and was patting the dog and talking to a guy who'd come out of the house. He turned around and waved at us to come on over there. Thebes and I got out of the van to see what was what. Adam told us the guy's name was Freak and we all introduced ourselves. Freak did the entire hand slapping, punching thing with Thebes, skilfully, and then also told her that he dug her hair and stylin' holster. And then he went over to the van for a look under the hood.

He's the real deal, said Adam. He'll fix it.

What's the dog's name? said Thebes.

Lucille, said Adam. After Freak's mom.

Freak came back over to us and said he'd have the van fixed in two hours, max, and we could hang out and do whatever we wanted while he worked.

How'd you get that fur and shit on your front bumper? he asked.

We hit a deer, I told him.

I'll Power Vac it off, he said. But I don't know if I can fix the dent. I told him there was a boy in the van and not to worry about him, he was afraid of Lucille.

Lucille's baked, said Freak. She loves everyone. But I don't really love her. She doesn't know it, though. I got her from a junkie who was going to rehab and couldn't keep her. I've only had her for like a week and she's already broken into my stash four times. Her name was The Beef, but I'm a vegan and I changed it.

Why? said Thebes. Were you going to eat her?

No way, man, said Freak, she's all muscle. That bitch is ripped. She's mellow now, though, but I still don't love her the way she deserves to be loved.

Well, said Thebes, what does she answer to better, The Beef or Lucille?

Neither, said Freak, she doesn't answer to anything. You can call her whatever you want.

I'm gonna call her Rajbeer, said Thebes.

After that kid in your class who doesn't know you're a person? I said.

Yeah, said Thebes.

Why? asked Adam.

Because I like his name, said Thebes, and because I really wanted to be friends with him.

Cool, said Freak. Rajbeer. He said he was gonna get to work on the van and we should make ourselves at home, his casa was our casa, and there was beer in the fridge.

Cherkis had tried to see the kids after Min had chased him down the street, screaming, with Thebes on her hip and me and Logan playing inferno in the backyard. He had sent letters and a bit of money, when he had it, and had tried to ask Min if she wanted him to take the kids for a while, or forever, so she could try to get her life together.

But every time she'd told him to go to hell, she could handle it on her own.

I tried to tell her that he only wanted to see them every once in a while, he was their dad, he missed them, he just wanted to say hi. He was trying to help. One time he showed up at their house and asked to see the kids and she freaked out and told him she'd call the cops and then called me and I had to go over there and ask him to leave and then she bundled the kids up, it was January or something, and put them in the car and they all drove away to one of her friends' places so Cherkis wouldn't be able to find them.

One Christmas I called him up in Tokyo. Min had told me that he was living there then, with another woman. I just wanted to ask him how he was doing and to tell him that the kids were fine, he didn't have to worry. He seemed pretty happy to hear from me and he asked some questions about the kids, like how were they doing at school, did they have friends, were they healthy, were they happy? Did Logan ever talk about him? Thebes was too young to remember him. I told him yeah, oh yeah, all that stuff, they're really good. I asked him how he was doing and he said he was all right, wanted to quit drinking quite so much, but all right. He didn't ask me how Min was, probably because it was too hard to hear the truth, and I didn't tell him, because it was also really hard to tell the truth.

Thebes wanted to hang with Freak and play with the dog, so Adam and I went into the house and wandered around

looking at things and being awkward with each other, saying things like, you're so great, no you are, no *you* are, and
then he suggested that I sit down with him on the couch
and look at Freak's crazy photo album of burned-out cars.
When I reached out to smooth the wrinkled plastic covering one of the shots, he put his hand on mine and then
some time passed and he was kissing me and I was melt-
ing into the couch and moving my hands around on his
back and through his tangled hair and then I stopped and
reminded him that he had a girlfriend and he said well,
yeah, kind of, but about a month ago he'd experimented
with quitting smoking pot and during that time, and it was
a *rough* three weeks, he'd realized how stupid she was.

Hey, c'mon, I said, that's not a nice thing to say, she
likes *you,* and he said that didn't really prove anything
but she was . . . whatever, *anyway,* we didn't need to stop,
did we?

Hey, I said, why don't you say some sexy things to me
in Sango or whatever that language is that you speak. I
told him it'd be great because I wouldn't understand what
I was missing and life was so much easier that way. He said
something interesting-sounding and oblique and I smiled
and nodded. He really wanted me to know what he had
said but I begged him not to translate. We messed around
sweetly and clumsily on Freak's grimy couch until Thebes
crashed through the front door.

Bonjourno! she said.

We flew to opposite ends of the couch like kids and
grinned at her like morons.

Hey, sweet crib, she said. What's shakin', homies?

Rajbeer was with her. And then Freak and Logan walked in, Freak had apparently convinced him that the dog was harmless, and then he went to the fridge and got everyone, except Thebes, a beer and told us the van was running like a top, cheers, wicked.

More difficult goodbyes. Adam asked for my phone number and I told him I didn't really have one right then. I didn't actually have a home, either, I told him.

Well, you're at home in the universe, he said.

Which universe? I said. I asked him for his number and he said it was disconnected.

Freak said I could call his place and leave a message for Adam if I felt like it and I wrote down his number on the back of a lottery ticket that had let him down months ago. Then Freak asked Thebes if she wanted to keep Lucille because Lucille needed love, and Logan and I put our hands up like stop, stop, stop, but it was way too late.

We were headed down the 40 West towards our final destination. Thebes was filthy all over again but who cares, she was alive, and Logan's cast was getting soggy and soft and fraying at the ends and I was aching with love or maybe something shallower and deeper at the same time for Adam, another guy I'd never see again in my life, and Rajbeer had eaten all the food Adam had made us and reeked like hell and wouldn't stop barking at the dying boy on the dash and we were all a little pissed off and sad and worried and silent. Except that, in spite of all that, I was also feeling kind of okay because I thought, I was pretty sure, I knew what I had to do and what I wanted to do.

You didn't call Min, said Logan.

And there was that. I was the world's worst guardian of children. I was like the neighbourhood cat lady, but with kids. They were filthy, broken and eating themselves and soon they'd feed on my old corpse. I had told them I'd phone their mother—after a really bad night of running away and being abandoned and cutting wrists, all they wanted was to talk to their mom—but instead I'd used that time to fool around with a disenfranchised American pothead.

Well, no, actually, I tried, I said. But I couldn't get through.

You did not, said Logan. Gimme a break.

I put in a CD and Logan took it out again and replaced it with one of his. It's my turn, he said. I've been keeping track. This is going out to Junkie. That was his name for Lucille/Rajbeer/The Beef. He cranked the volume on "Atomic Dog." Do you like George Clinton? he asked me.

Yeah, I do, I said. He told me he was thinking of starting a band when he got home and calling it The Missed Appointments.

Good name, I said. Do you play an instrument? He said he could play a few chords on the guitar, nothing much.

Hey, said Thebes, did you write this? She was talking to Logan, waving a green piece of construction paper around. It turned out he'd played Poetry Class with her after all and had written a poem while he was in the van hiding out from the dog.

Can I read it out loud? she asked him.

No, he said. Give me that. He tried to grab it but she yanked it away. Fuck off, Thebes, he said. Give it to me. She started to read. He swore and disappeared into his hoodie.

Bury 22 footers (in your eye)
Run the floor
Elevate, finish the deuce
Move the feet, lock it down
Box out
Rise up
Start the break
Hard dribble, pull up (on your head).
Forearm to the chest
Finish with the left
Hard pick, knock you off your feet.
Box out
Rise up
Put back
Shake your head
Jab step, release (in your face)
Get low (put a body on 'em)
Board with one hand
Dribble, spin, fade
It's a beautiful thing.

It's a basketball poem! said Thebes.

Give me that, said Logan. Please? He grabbed it from her and tore it up, and then opened the window and threw out the pieces.

Why did you do that? I said. That was a good poem.

Whatever, said Logan.

The rain had started again and it was foggy. I'd forgotten to ask Freak if he could fix the windshield wiper.

We should try to tie the shirt around the thing again, I said.

I can do it, said Logan.

I pulled over and Logan grabbed the T-shirt and got out of the van. Stay in here, Thebes, it's raining, I said.

I took a plastic bag out of the back and joined Logan outside. I asked him to put the bag over his cast so it wouldn't get wet and decompose but he said it would be okay, it wasn't raining that hard. It sure was foggy, though. I told Logan that I had really liked his poem and that he shouldn't have thrown it away. He didn't say anything. He was trying hard to wrap the T-shirt around the wiper blade so that it wouldn't fly off.

You know? I said. He was quiet. Hey, I said. What . . . are you crying?

He ignored me and kept working on the wiper. The T-shirt wouldn't stop slipping off the blade and semis were spraying water all over us as they passed and the earth shook every time. Logan stopped fiddling around with the wiper and turned to look at me.

This is so messed up, he said. He *was* crying.

I put my arms around him and told him things would be okay, we'd figure it out, Min would get better, but he just shook his head and said he didn't know. Thebes was looking at us through the window.

Let's go over here, I said, and took Logan's hand and led him through the ditch and up onto the other side and through a hole in an electric fence into an empty field. We sat on a rock in the rain and he cried and I tried to think of something to say that would comfort him, something true.

I know it wasn't my mom's idea for us to find Cherkis, said Logan. I've known that all along.

Yeah? I said. Okay. You're right, it wasn't. It was my idea and I'm really sorry for lying to you. I really am. I thought this was the best thing to do. The only thing I could think of was finding Cherkis and asking him to take care of you guys so at least . . . I don't know. It was probably a stupid idea but I was desperate.

I don't know either, said Logan. It's messed up.

Yeah, it is, I said. Right now it is, but it won't always be.

I kind of think it always will be, said Logan.

Yeah, I know, I said. It seems that way, but—

No, it really is that way, he said. He was crying hard, trying to talk. Even when she gets better, he said, it's for like three days or maybe a week and then it's over, she gives up, it's just so . . . I think Thebes and I are on our own.

No, no, I said. You're not on—

Yeah, said Logan, we are. I don't know how to take care of a kid, but she's my sister, so . . . that's that. I can get a job somewhere, I think. I'll be sixteen in a month.

I know, I said, but . . . that's not . . . You're not on your own.

Hat, I'm not stupid, said Logan. You can go back to Paris, or wherever, you don't have to take care of us. I've got it.

Let's go back to the van, I said. C'mon. I pulled him up off the rock and he smiled and said I had a pretty decent grip. Let's get out of here, I said.

But the van wasn't there, and the fog was so thick I could barely see Logan's face. Jesus Christ, I said. Oh god. Oh man. What the . . . why . . . ?

Did you leave the keys in the van? asked Logan.

I was kneeling on the side of the highway, holding onto my head like a prisoner of war.

Thebes! Logan yelled her name once and then again and then he started running down the highway and quickly disappeared in the fog.

A minute later I saw the van reversing towards me. It stopped and Logan jumped out and ran around to where I was sitting and helped me up. He opened up the passenger side door and shoved me in. Thebes was sitting in the back seat with her arm around the dog.

Good one, eh? she said. No? Who knew I could drive?

Min and I were kids. Our parents had rented a cottage at some lake. There was a long dock and Min ran the length of it and leaped into the water and disappeared. My parents and I stood on the dock screaming her name. My father jumped into the water but couldn't find her and our mother ran to the cottage to phone the search and rescue. Twenty minutes later Min poked her head out from under the dock. There'd been six inches or so of space between the wooden planks and the water and she'd hid there listening to us go crazy looking for her. She didn't get it. She couldn't understand how or why we'd be angry because damn it, it was so funny, so smooth.

That night she and I lay in our bunk beds and I asked her if she wouldn't have panicked if it had been me hiding under the dock and she didn't know where I was because the last thing she'd seen of me was me jumping into the water, and she said yeah, she would have panicked. She told me there was only one person in the world she loved and that person was me.

The rain had stopped and the fog had lifted. Min, I said to myself, we're here. Do we keep going? I didn't know what else to say. I tried to remember the Uncertainty Principle but couldn't. I waited for her to answer. I told myself that if in ten seconds I looked out the window and happened to see water, I would know that Min had answered. No, I thought, I'm going to change that to a tree. We were in a really dry part of the United States. No, I thought, actually we're in a desert, I'm going to change it to a cactus. No, wait, a bird. I counted to ten. I looked out the window and thought for sure, definitely, I had just seen some type of flying creature. Yes, I had. It was a giant circling vulture and he had many friends and they were closing in on the shredded carcass of half a cow. Still. I would consider the vulture to be Min's answer. I didn't know what dark meaning it held, but maybe, hopefully, none.

———

When Logan was a little kid he would run away from home. He'd go outside and hide behind the giant elm in their front yard. Sometimes he'd stand there for hours, waiting to be found.

One time Min and the kids and I were having lunch in a restaurant. Thebes was in a high chair having a fit over something and Min and I were trying to get her to calm down. When she finally did, Logan was gone. He'd left a note, spelled out in square letters along the edge of a round coaster. I have run away for the 3 time, it said. We ran out of the restaurant and found him halfway down the block watching a busker perform magic tricks. I still have the coaster somewhere. I should give it to Min, or Logan. It was a coaster advertising some coffee with the words "Select Discoveries" in the centre.

Let's stop for gas, I said. Thebes was in the back, building something, quietly singing a Smokey Robinson tune, "I Second That Emotion," and the dog was asleep on the floor. The water in the cooler sloshed around so much that if we didn't have music playing it sounded like we were in a small fishing boat on a slightly choppy lake. I imagine that it's the boat in Logan's dream, the one that we're all in, out at sea, and my father pops up from the water with his glasses on and says how happy he is to see us.

Logan careened into the parking lot of the gas station, filled the van up and then dribbled his basketball around for a while. Thebes zipped into the washroom and I could hear her singing in there while I stood and paid at the counter. Kid's happy, said the clerk. She came out and I bought her an Archie comic, and when we were walking back to the van I asked her what she was thinking about.

I don't know, she said.

C'mon, you do so, I said.

I'm just wondering if Cherkis is going to like me, she said.

Heads up, T., said Logan. Thebes rammed her Archie into her mouth to free up her hands and caught the ball like a pro and fired it right back at him. The side door on the van was open and Rajbeer leapt out all caught up in the excitement of the game and then one of the gas station employees came out and asked us please to put that pit bull away and also no playing in the parking lot, because they get a lot of tour buses full of seniors who enjoy serenity when they disembark.

While Logan drove, I put my feet on the dash. The world whipped past us. You should slow down a bit, I told Logan. Thebes lay down in the back and said she wanted to think about things for a while but if something earth-shattering happened we should let her know. Then she said all right, she was finished thinking about things and she started reading us stuff about Kingman from an Arizona travel book she'd picked up along the way.

Did you know, she said, that Kingman is the site of BLEVE. The Boiling Liquid Expanding Vapour Explosion?

No, neither Logan or I were aware of that.

Firefighters from around the world study it, said Thebes. And did you know, she said, that Pamela Anderson did one of her *Playboy* photo shoots at the corner of Fourth Street and Andy Devine Avenue and was brought into the Kingman Police Department for indecent exposure?

Really? said Logan.

No, I didn't know that either, I said.

She wasn't charged, said Thebes, but she was asked to write a letter of apology.

Yeah, they must have been really mad, said Logan. Are there photos in that book?

No, said Thebes, only maps.

Did the Pamela Lee Anderson thing coincide with the expanding liquid explosion thing? he asked.

It doesn't say, said Thebes. I don't think so.

There was something about Thebes not twigging to Logan's dirty joking that made me want to cry, made me think of Min and me as kids and made me want to travel backwards but not exactly back to where we'd come from.

And did you know, she said, that Kingman is called the Heart of Historic Route 66? The longest original stretch of Route 66 runs right through downtown Kingman. It's called the Mother Road. Thebes liked that. The Mother Road. But she didn't know what Route 66 was. Neither did Logan, really.

Don't you guys know the song? I asked them. You know, "Get your kicks on Route 66 . . ."?

Drawing a blank, said Logan.

Kicks? said Thebes, do you mean, like, shoes?

fifteen

WE WERE SITTING IN A NAUGAHYDE BOOTH in a restaurant in Kingman. I ordered a large pot of coffee for myself and the kids played Hangman while we waited for our food. Our waitress told us this was her last shift because later that day she was going to get on a plane for the very first time and fly all the way over to North Carolina to hook up with a guy she'd met online.

Her friends had all told her she was crazy to do it but she didn't care, she hadn't even purchased cancellation insurance for the flight. She'd given up her apartment.

So, then, do you think you'll stay there forever? I asked her.

If all goes according to plan, yeah, she said.

And this'll be the first time you meet him in person? I asked.

Yeah, she said. Do you want to see a picture of him? She took a tiny photo out of her apron pocket and handed it to me.

Oh, he's really cute, I said. And he seems nice? I passed the photo to Logan, who didn't look at it, just passed it to Thebes, who stared at it.

Oh, yeah! said the waitress. Real nice. I'm so excited I keep spilling things, I'm sorry.

Hey, no problem, I said. It's understandable. I hope it all works out.

Yeah, thanks, she said. It just . . . really has to this time.

Thebes handed the waitress her photo. What do you mean *this* time? she said. What happened last time? Do you want to sit down?

Logan astrally projected himself out of there and I gave Thebes a tiny kick under the table.

No, said the waitress, thanks, but I have to keep working.

Yeah, but, said Thebes, why didn't your last relation-ship work out?

Oh, you know, said the waitress.

No, said Thebes.

Oh, well, you know, she said, there were certain things that he wanted that I just couldn't give him.

The waitress looked at me and asked me if she could tell Thebes something straight up.

Yeah, of course, I said. I was waiting for the worst type of confession, something that would send Thebes racing to her dictionary to look up fist-fucking or dirty sanchez.

He really wanted a baby, she said.

And you didn't? said Thebes.

No, she said, I really did too, but my Fallopian tubes were scarred from an abortion I had when I was eighteen and now I can't get pregnant.

Oh, I said, that's too bad, I'm sorry.

Yeah, that blows, said Thebes.

Yeah, said the waitress. But, so, now, this new guy? He doesn't care about babies. He doesn't want them. He just wants me.

Oh, that's so sweet, I said. You're lucky. Sounds like he's—

Yeah, but, said Thebes, so what happens if you do, somehow, end up getting pregnant with this new guy and then you have this baby and the new guy still doesn't want one?

Thebes, I said. That's not—

Yeah, no, said the waitress. She was smiling. I won't get pregnant, she said. I don't have a uterus any more.

What! said Thebes. Why not?

Logan had by now asphyxiated himself with his hood.

The waitress told us about her hysterectomy and then said she had to go, she was getting dirty looks from her boss.

Yeah, but, said Thebes, he's only gonna be your boss for five more minutes or something, who cares? Let's talk. She slapped her hands down on the table, palms up, like, *go ahead, fill me up with your stories of reckless gynecology,* and I caught a glimpse of the faint, so-called meaningless scratches on the inside of her wrists.

No, the waitress had to go. I said good luck in North Carolina. Thebes got up and gave her a hug and told her to keep it real. Keep it strong. She hoped the guy turned out to be as sweet as he looked in his photo and would never want to have a baby.

I decided to call Marc. I'd been trying in countless futile ways to disengage, to detach and drift away from him, from thoughts of him, but I was having moments, like this one now, where he managed to slip back in and wrap himself around my brain and there was nothing I could do about it. I thought I loved him. I think I did love him. I wanted him to love me, I knew that. But that may not be the definition of love, wanting someone else to love you and *then* deciding whether you love them back. Logan and Thebes were racing backwards in the ditch. They had let Rajbeer out of the steaming hot van and tied her up to the bumper so she could lie in the shade. Seniors were roaming around the parking lot in slow-moving packs, propping each other up and taking tiny, tiny steps like they were walking on tightropes.

Marc?

Yeah. Hey . . . hey! How are you? Wow!

Fine. How are you?

I've been trying to reach you, he said.

What? Oh! You mean telepathically?

Yeah!

Really? I didn't . . .

You didn't sense it?

Um, not really, I don't think so . . . What were you saying?

I was saying I really miss you, you know?

Really? No, I . . . no, I wasn't getting that at all . . . but, really? You do?

Yeah.

Well, and . . . hmm . . .

Are you at your sister's? he asked.

No, I'm in Arizona, I said.

Why?

Because it's on the way to California.

An old man tapped me on the shoulder and asked me if I'd be much longer on the phone. I shook my head and held up two fingers. The man nodded but didn't move.

Are you going to California? said Marc.

Yes, yeah, sort of . . . I miss you too. I smiled at the old guy and he patted my shoulder and smiled back at me again, a little sadly, maybe with some turn-of-the-century memory he couldn't shake, like of a World War I candystriper. Or maybe he just really wanted to use the phone.

What are you doing in California? asked Marc.

The old guy puckered his lips and blew me a kiss and

nodded knowingly and pointed at the phone. I smiled again and shook my head.

Oh, nothing, I said. Well, some things. Just . . . checking it out. Mining for gold. What are you doing?

So Marc's new relationship had worked out and then it had stopped working out and now he wanted me back. He wanted me to return to Paris and we'd start fresh, with less weirdness and more honesty. This was the perfect opportunity for a homeless woman with low self-esteem and mild addiction issues. He did tell me he loved me and I told him that I appreciated that, as though he had offered to carry my grocery bags out to the car. He asked me if I loved him too, and I told him I didn't really know. I wanted to say yes but I wasn't sure. He considered that for a few seconds and then he asked me if I thought that maybe, in time, I would love him again, because hadn't I loved him once and wasn't that proof that it could reoccur. I told him I wasn't sure that he was the one I was supposed to be loving at the moment and he said that love didn't work that way, we didn't choose who to love or when to love. I told him he was probably right, ninety-nine per cent. We left it at that, more or less. He asked me to call him again when I got a chance and I told him I'd try to. He asked me what I wanted him to do with all my psychology textbooks if I decided I wasn't coming back. Well, you could read them, I told him. Or give them away. I didn't care. I was planning to develop my own form of psychotherapy, like Freud or Jung. Marc was skeptical. He reminded me that I had no formal training in the field of psychiatry. I know, I said. That's true. I told him I was planning to save my sister's life, but that I needed a bit more time to figure out just how. Is she dying? he asked me. Yes, I said. He said he was very sorry but that I was sounding a little crazy and should probably leave her care in the hands of medical professionals. I know, I said, that's a very rational and time-proven theory, but I don't think it's going to work this time.

We were driving out of Kingman and Logan saw an ancient basketball court next to a bombed-out school. We stopped so he could shoot hoops for fifteen minutes and I could smoke a cigarette outside the van, new Theban rule. We let Rajbeer run around. Thebes and I took turns pushing each other around in circles on one of those old-timey, spinny wooden things. I sat cross-legged in the centre, smoking, feeling nauseous, but also, in spite of spinning around in circles, quite focused. Thebes ran faster and faster until she was practically horizontal, and then she flung herself on and sat next to me while we spun around and around and around and then slowly, slowly, came to a stop. After that we walked over to the court and I lay in the grass next to it and Thebes stood on the sidelines coaching Logan.

Get open, Troutman! she yelled. Box out! Baseline! Arms up! Arms *up!* Do I have to get down on my knees and pray? Who's your man!

Logan was trying not to laugh.

Keep your head in the game! Stay with your man! Christ! Do I have to get out my dictionary and show you the definition of *open?* Who do you have, Troutman, who do you have?

Logan stopped shooting and came over to where Thebes and I were standing.

What do you think about when you shoot? I asked him.

Nothing, he said.

Oh, really? I said. You just concentrate entirely on shooting?

Yeah, I guess, he said.

Do you worry that the ball won't go in? I asked him.

No, he said, I always believe that it will. Every time.

Seriously? I said. Even when you've missed a bunch of shots?

Yeah, I think it's gonna go in every time, he said.

And then, so, when it doesn't go in do you feel all disillusioned? I asked him.

No, not at all, he said, 'cause I'm always sure the next one will go in.

From Kingman we dipped down, straight south, and drove through a town called Needles, childhood home of Charles M. Schulz and a pit stop for the Joad Family in *The Grapes of Wrath*. We kept on driving and then dropped farther south to a narrow, virtually empty road through the desert that would take us right into Twentynine Palms. It was over a hundred degrees, even with the sun going down, the AC was on full blast, the highway was shimmering and the shadows were rippling like waves. Tiny rodents ran back and forth along the highway and I tried really hard not to hit them.

The kids were yawning and falling asleep, the dog had been fed and was quiet and staring out the back window, the boy's head was back on the dash—Thebes had made him a hat, too, a pirate hat—the cooler had been restocked with ice, and it really was getting late.

Our family once went on a road trip and my father drove two hundred miles in the wrong direction. The moment of realization, for him, was a low point in the holiday. I had seen him defeated on many occasions but this was the major leagues. Min and I, for some reason, not because we enjoyed seeing our father suffer, not at all, but because it didn't really matter to us where we were going, thought it was the funniest thing that could ever have happened. While our dad stared at the map in disbelief, our mother took us aside and said okay, girls, I know you're going to want to laugh until you throw up, but let's all try to think about how Dad feels and keep a lid on it. If you can't help yourselves, please pretend that you're laughing at something else. So for two hours Min and I pretended we were laughing at unfunny things like clouds and trees and fences until finally our father said to our mother, are those two complete morons or what?

Is that supposed to be a story? asked Thebes.

Well, I don't know, I said. What did you want? I panic when you ask for a story.

Okay, said Logan, was that last part supposed to be

like a joke? Because if it was, we'd need more information, just a tiny bit, like about how Grandpa, said it, what he was implying, you know what I mean?

Okay, I said, yeah, by asking if Min and I were morons, Grandpa was making fun of himself for having driven in the wrong direction for so long. He was acknowledging that he had been the moron and that now it could all be funny and we could all just relax. That is what I was trying to convey. And that it was sweet of him to let us off the hook like that.

Okay, said Logan, then cool. I think it kind of works.

God, I feel like I'm defending my Ph.D. thesis, I said.

Did you even finish your B.A.? asked Thebes.

I smiled and told her to shut up.

I had this dream, she said. I was talking to Min on the phone but while I was talking to her I could hear this other person talking about something totally different at the same time, and then I figured out that the other person was also me, but I didn't really like that me. And then I decided to take the bus to the hospital and see Min but when I got there my other self was already there.

Logan and I were quiet for a few seconds.

Thebes, said Logan, you should stop using hair dye. That shit can seep into the brain.

A tube of LePage's glue flew around the van for a while, front to the back, front to the back. Rajbeer threw up a ball of duct tape and a marker cap.

After a few minutes Thebes said she had a problem. She said she didn't know, now, if she really wanted to see Cherkis after all. It was making her too nervous. She didn't know how she felt. She was confused. She said we'd come all this way and now she was wondering if it might be okay if she didn't see him and was I mad. I told her I wasn't mad and that she could see him or not see him, it was her choice. She could do exactly as she pleased.

Whatever you want, Thebie, I said. You don't have to decide right now.

We got to Twentynine Palms in the middle of the night and checked into a motel. Thebes had fallen asleep in the van and wouldn't wake up, so Logan and I carried her in, he took her legs, I took her arms, like we were going to count to three and throw her into the pool. We had to sneak Rajbeer in too, under the sign that said No Pets or Parties Allowed.

Logan and I sat at the table in the room in the dark and smoked a joint while Thebes and Rajbeer slept.

So what if he's not actually here? said Logan.

I don't know, I said.

We both started to laugh, quietly. Then we stopped, and then we started again.

sixteen

HEY, MIN, I WHISPERED. The kids were sleeping and the sun was rising. I'd finally managed to get through to her.

Hattie? she said. It was only my name but hearing her say it killed me.

Yeah, I said. Yeah, it's me.

How are you? she said. How are the kids?

We're all great, I said. How are you? Are you okay?

Yeah, she said. I'm all right.

Really? I said. You are?

Yeah, she said. Well, you know . . . yeah, I'm fine. The kids are okay?

Totally, I said. They're great. They're fine. They miss you like crazy.

I miss them too, said Min.

I know, I said. Hey, is Superman still your roommate?

No, she said, Lex Luthor came around and . . .

Yeah, yeah, I said.

They're really okay? she said.

They are, Min, they really, really are. Rock solid. You too?

I am, yeah, she said. I'm fine . . . well, you know, I'm here . . . but yeah, I'm fine. You're sure they're all right, Hattie? said Min. Are you telling me the truth?

Positive, I said. I'd let you talk to them but they're sleeping right now.

But it's . . . Shouldn't they be getting ready for school?

What? I said. Oh, yeah! Damn. You're right. I should get on that.

I promised myself this would be the last time, or very close to the last time, that I would lie to Min.

Okay, but, Hattie? said Min.

Yeah? I said.

They said I could probably go home soon.

Really? I said. That's fantastic! That's great. Wow. That's really great.

Yeah, said Min. I seem to have gotten through to the second lieutenant. But they'll only discharge me if there's someone at home to help out.

Yeah, I said. Oh, yeah. Well, yeah! I'll be there, obviously, right? I mean, of course I will be.

Are you at home? said Min.

Mmmhmm, I said.

We listened to each other breathing. I heard someone coughing on her end. I heard some other things.

Hey, um, Min? I said.

Yeah, she said.

Why aren't you at the beach? I said.

Nice, she said, why aren't you?

Good question, I said. I'll meet you there.

Where?

At the beach.

Okay, she said, which beach?

You know the one, that very large one with all the sand, I said.

Oh, yeah . . . , she said, the one next to all that water?

Yeah, that one.

Sounds good, said Min. Sounds like a plan.

Scissor-kick, I said.

I am, she said.

Like crazy? I said. Ha ha?

Shut up . . . yeah, she said.

I am, too, I said.

We should maybe float on our backs for a minute or two, she said. Like, rest . . .

Yeah . . . I said. Very soon. We should try to get a little bit closer first . . .

More breathing, more treading. I heard a public announcement, something about breakfast being over in five minutes. I heard Min's name being called.

What the hell is that? I asked her. You're being paged?

They want me to eat, she said.

Oh, I said. You should go?

I guess so, she said.

Or like forty lashes or something? I said.

Worse, she said, I'd have to share.

Oh, like in Group?

Yep, she said.

You fail breakfast, I said.

I know, said Min. I fail Crafts, too, spectacularly.

Yeah, I said, I hear those skills skip a generation. Thebes is a master.

Yeah, said Min, what's her latest project? Has she made you a novelty-sized cheque yet?

No, not yet. She's more into performance art lately. I looked over at the kids, both fast asleep.

I told Min I'd call her later, the kids were great, the kids were happy, the kids were aces, and we'd all be reunited in the sweet by and by when we met on that beautiful shore . . .

Twentynine Palms is the proud host of the Marine Corps Air Ground Combat Center, the world's largest marine base, said Thebes as we were getting ready to check out.

Fuckin' A, I said.

We're meat, said Logan. And it's pronounced "core," dufus, not "corpse."

We had to hurry. Thebes said yeah, now she did want to meet Cherkis, she felt better about it. She'd put on her least filthy outfit, the royal blue terry cloth shorts and top. Her hair was by now impossible to comb. But it didn't matter.

Hey, do you ever brush your teeth? I asked her. She had her holster on, she'd patted her face a couple of times with a dry washcloth, whatever, she hated water. She leaned against the wall and said she was ready.

So, here we go, said Logan. Cherkis hunting. Let's do this thing. He was using his knife to scratch inside his cast. His hickeys had faded to green and yellow and had all bled together so it looked like he'd recently been strangled. I felt like I had an ice pick stuck between my eyes, I could barely open them, it was the mother of all headaches, and I couldn't take a breath without paroxysms of pain shooting from my brain to my chest and back again.

We were going to hit an art gallery on the main drag first to see if anyone there had heard the name Cherkis. While we were loading our crap back into the van, Rajbeer got out and ran around the parking lot, barking and pissing everywhere. A little girl, about three, came up to Logan and pointed at Rajbeer and asked, Can I ride she?

Her, said Logan, and no, I'm sorry, but I don't really think so. Thebes was trying to round up the dog and this girl wouldn't stop talking to Logan, about her socks, about her blanket, about her Barbies, about her grandma, about her baby brother, about her nightmares, about how her socks bothered her ankles, about a boy in her daycare named Ed. Thebes had wrangled Rajbeer into the van by now and I wanted to go.

Hey, do you have parents around here or something? I asked the girl. She pointed at the motel. Where? I said. Like, which room? She stared at me. Oh, for Christ's sake.

I asked her to come with me and I took her hand and we started knocking on doors. One opened and the guy said yeah and I said is this your kid and he said no. She didn't belong in the next three rooms either. Finally, a woman opened a door and said yeah, oh, sorry, the girl was hers, she did this all the time, thanks a lot.

Twentynine Palms, said Thebes, would be fourteen people with their hands out, going what? What? And one with one hand in his or her pocket.

Do we have anything to eat? asked Logan. Thebes fished around in the cooler and threw him a giant Oh Henry! bar.

I don't see any soldiers, said Thebes.

They're in foxholes, I said. I was in such a hurry, I was bumping into curbs and slamming my brakes down at the last second for red lights that jumped out of nowhere.

Shit, I'm burning, I said. I had dropped my cigarette but hadn't bothered to find out where. Logan reached over and grabbed it and threw it out the window.

Do you want me to—

Yes!

Logan and I switched seats and he drove. His driving was improving but he still had this tendency to sail through stop signs and red lights. I told him to concentrate on seeing other cars and especially pedestrians and then slowly ease into seeing signs as well. And remember to brake going into the turn, gas going out.

Thought the rule was no smoking in the van, he said. Are you still burning?

I'm trying to stay calm, I said.

I appreciate the effort, he said.

Thebes had on her giant diamond necklace and she'd found her angel ring. What foxholes? she said.

You're looking for somebody by the name of Cherkis? said the woman at the gallery.

Yeah, Doug Cherkis, I said. I was told that he might have been doing his art around here somewhere, or running a gallery, or something like that? I put my elbow on her desk so I could prop my head up and I squinted at her. Ring any bells? I asked. The kids were studying some abstracts on a long, white wall.

I'm so sorry, said the woman. You know, I just can't . . . That name is not at all familiar to me.

Really? I said. Would it be all right if I poured myself some of that coffee?

Oh, of course, she said. I'll get it. Would you like cream or sugar?

No, thanks, black is great.

Doug Cherkis, said the woman. Doug Cherkis. You know, a friend of mine might know if there was a Doug Cherkis around here. The woman gave us directions to her friend's place, she had a studio in her house and it wasn't very far from the gallery. Her name was Lilah.

I thanked her and she wished us luck.

Hey, kids, I said. Van. March, I said. I looked at the woman. Did I just say "march"? I asked her. She smiled and shrugged. She lived in a town filled with soldiers.

Oh, your cup, I said.

Take it, she said. She told me I could keep it as a souvenir.

I thanked her and we left.

On the way over to Lilah's I whipped into a Discount Everything to buy a few groceries and some more pain-killers. The kids played Frisbee in the parking lot while I shopped. It was subarctic in there, air-conditioned down to zero. I had to keep moving or I'd freeze to death. I raced up and down the aisles throwing discounted every-thing into my cart, trying to maintain my circulation and stay alive. It's fun to be challenged, I guess, to have even the well-documented evidence that human beings need a certain body temperature to sustain life discounted. On the way back to the van I saw a piece of paper lying on the ground with the word *Faith* written on it in big letters, so I picked it up. I turned the paper over and realized that it was an Account Close Authorization for a Miss Faith Mae Hopkins. I put it in my pocket anyway.

It took us three minutes to get to Lilah's place. Thebes and Logan argued about how much the window should be left open for Rajbeer not to suffocate to death from the heat. Logan said he'd wait in the van this time. Okay, I said, but I made him promise he wouldn't take off.

Thebes and I went into the house/studio, a groovy space, the walls painted orange and purple and covered in goofy art. A girl, maybe a little younger than Thebes, said, Hey, what's up? *Buenos días!* She'd been sitting cross-legged on the hardwood floor, spinning herself around in circles.

Bonjourno! said Thebes. They stared at each other and grinned.

Yo, Mom! yelled the girl. We are not alone!

A blonde woman came out of a room in the back and said hello and welcome. She looked at Thebes. I looked at the other girl. We were all staring at each other and grinning.

You totally know Doug Cherkis, don't you? I said to the woman.

So, yeah, turned out the kids had a half-sister, almost an exact replica of Thebes but about two years younger. A sophisticated nine, she said. Her name was Antonia. She took Thebes outside to show her some stuff and then Logan shot hoops with them behind their garage, laughing his head off as these two little look-alike girls, his sisters, tried to block and tackle him.

But Cherkis wasn't there. And when he *had* been there he'd gone by the name Charles instead. Doug Charles.

Do you think that's because he didn't want to be found? I asked Lilah.

No, she said, he just thought Cherkis sounded dumb, I think.

She told me that about five or six months ago he'd

gone to a place called Calexico, a border town, which was near a Mexican town called Mexicali. They weren't really talking much any more. Doug is a bit of a loner, she said. I asked her if he'd ever mentioned Min and the kids and Lilah said yeah, he had a couple of times, but he hadn't gone into much detail.

He kept a lot of pictures of her, though, said Lilah. He didn't show them to me, but I found them in one of his boxes. They looked really happy together. Then Lilah told me that she thought the reason she and Cherkis had never really connected in a big way was that he was still in love with Min.

Do you really think so? I asked her.

Well, she said, he was always distracted. He was sweet, and he was great with Antonia, but he would often stare out the window like he was expecting someone to show up any minute. You know, he'd stare at planes whenever they flew over, he'd disappear for periods of time. Once he told me he was planning on going on a road trip to Canada but I guess he changed his mind.

Lilah told me that Cherkis had gone to the border to join a group of anarchists or something who were committed to keeping track of and documenting the actions and injustices of the U.S. Border Patrol.

How far is it from here? I said.

Maybe a hundred and fifty miles? she said. You'd go straight south through Joshua Tree National Park.

Does he have a phone number that you know of? I said.

No, not that I know of, she said. They have two-way radios. They're living in tents in a kind of no-man's land.

Sometimes he'll call from a phone booth if he goes into town, to talk to Antonia.

But do any kids live there? I said.

In the town? she said.

No, like with the people in the tents, I said. Is it possible?

She didn't know. Maybe. Why not? But there wouldn't be much for them to do.

When the girls came back into the house they were talking non-stop. Thebes was telling Antonia a story about dancing.

Logan and I went to our community centre sports banquet, she said, and he got a bunch of awards and I won a deflated basketball for participation and wore my little black dress from my neighbour and some of her old high heels and a black choker and danced with a boy named Dang. There's a tall Dang and a short Dang, she said. I danced with the short Dang but Logan said I should have danced with the tall Dang. Logan sat at a different table with his friends and then danced weirdly, like a robot, and then left in a green car full of girls.

Then Antonia told Thebes about her grandma's birthday party.

We had a nice birthday party for Grandma, she said, even though we forgot to get her the one thing she had asked for, which was a splatter lid for her frying pan. Then we took her to a play. *Romeo and Juliet*. It was really good except it was interactive so we had to keep hauling Grandma out of her little foldy chair so we could move around to the various scenes. I really liked it. The guy who played Juliet's dad had the palest blue eyes that I've ever seen. When I told Mom that Benvolio and Paris sure looked a lot alike, she said yeah, I guess that's because they're the same guy.

This cracked them both up and they had the same throaty laugh. I guess they must have inherited it from Cherkis but it had been a long time since I'd heard him laugh. I could remember him crying, though, at their dining room table. He cried a lot in the last few months he was with Min. She'd barricade herself in the bathroom or in the basement and he and I would maintain a type of vigil, I guess, sharing a bottle of bourbon and waiting for Min to come out of hiding.

Thebes and Antonia kept talking. They were unstoppable. Thebes told Antonia that her grandma, when she was alive, played Scrabble on ships for money and Antonia told Thebes that her grandma was shrivelled up and had just won three hundred bucks at Bingo.

She has these tiny photos of people in frames, said Antonia, like of her husband and her grandchildren and stuff and she puts them in a half-circle around her Bingo cards and dabbers.

Cool, said Thebes. Like, for luck?

Yeah, said Antonia, and she calls me Nevada.

Hey, Thebie, I said, we should really think about hitting the road, eh?

Hey, said Antonia, do you wanna play Trouble?

Yeah! said Thebes. But first do you want to hear my Satan voice?

She did. Then Antonia told Thebes that the riot police, the ones with shields, had just stormed a house on their street and kicked in the back door but the person they were looking for wasn't there and they had to apologize.

Hey, said Thebes, have you ever been to a meat fair? Do you know what mad cow disease is? All our cows in Canada went crazy and a bunch of farmers had a meat fair at the ballpark and sold hamburger for like a dollar a pound.

Make it a fast game, okay? I said.

Lilah and I talked more about Cherkis. She said she had never really got him. She had tried to get inside him but she felt she'd never succeeded. She said talking to him sometimes made her feel like a grave robber.

While we talked and the girls played Trouble, Logan used a sledgehammer to smash up the sidewalk in the front yard. Lilah had asked him if he wanted to because she was planning to put in a new one. She opened the window and a hot breeze blew in and she called to him that he was doing a great job.

This'll be my legacy, he said.

Smashing the obvious and well-worn paths that lead us from one place to another, I thought. Go Logan.

I'd come up with a plan. Min was in the universe. She was a dim and falling star, but she was alive. She hadn't loved watching the sun's eclipse as much as she'd loved watching it reappear. If she had really, truly wanted to die she'd have succeeded a long time ago. She loved the brink, going to it and returning from it. Or maybe she didn't love it. Maybe she hated it. But it didn't matter. Maybe going to the brink made her feel like she'd accomplished something extraordinary, like there was a purpose to her life, if only to prolong it in spite of herself. She was the captain of both teams, waging war against herself but always pulling back from any decisive victory because that would also mean a decisive loss.

I had a new career. I had a mission. I'd become a cartographer of the uncharted world of Min and I'd raise her from the dead, like a baby, sort of. We'd do it from scratch. We'd start all over. When she was well enough to take control, she could throw me out, plot her own course, and I wouldn't stand in her way. And I wouldn't help her to die.

I had faith in my plan. I had faith in Min. And I loved her. She was the baby in my dreams and maybe in Logan's too. If Logan had faith that he'd make his shot every time, even when the misses were piling up, I could have faith that my next attempt at saving Min would be the one that worked.

And then, according to the tao of Logan, if it didn't, so what, I'd try again and believe one hundred per cent that the next one would.

seventeen

I DROVE THROUGH THE PARK as fast as I could, which was excruciatingly slowly because the road was narrow and curvy and park rangers were all over the place. It was all desert and sky and scrubby bushes and some oddly shaped trees.

The Joshua tree is named after a biblical story in which Joshua reaches his hands up to the sky to stop the sun by God's command, said Thebes. Why would God want the sun stopped?

Have you noticed how freaking hot it is out here? said Logan.

We talked about the strangeness of a day in which you find a sister you never knew you had *and* meet your father, who was once an artist and is now some sort of vigilante.

Before parting, Thebes and Antonia had promised to write and e-mail and do amazing things together someday. Antonia told Thebes they could go to Burning Man when they were older, or Disneyland or the Leaning Tower of Pisa or whatever, and she gave Logan a guitar that she'd found in the garbage but that still worked. He asked her to sign his cast. Thebes made Antonia a kite with stuff she had in the back of the van. She'd drawn a picture of herself on it, waving and smiling. Lilah took a few Polaroids of all of us and gave them to us to keep.

When we were in the van, Thebes put her arms around Logan's neck from behind and said, Don't you love having *two* little sisters?

I braced myself for the inevitable *yeah, like I love being hung upside down by my nuts* and *Chinese water torture,* or whatever, but instead Logan turned around and smiled at her and mussed her hair and said yeah, he did, but she, Thebes, would always be his favourite.

She kept her arms around Logan's neck for a long time and he didn't tell her to stop.

Hey, Thebes, I said.

Yo.

Can you make me a kite like the one you made for Antonia? I too wanted to see Thebes waving at me from the sky, top star in the firmament, goofy on the earth *and* up above it.

Can do, daddio, she said, and flung herself backwards into her pool of art supplies.

Logan, I whispered.

What? he said. He was whispering too.

I love you, I said.

Fuck off, he said, smiling.

I put my hand on his knee because I didn't know what else to do and he touched it briefly with his own, unbroken one.

We were out of the park, flying down the 86 South towards the U.S.–Mexico border, past the Salton Sea, which was really a lake, man-made, I think, and crawling with pelicans. I remembered Min trying to befriend a pelican on this beach that was next to the campground we stayed in one summer. She pretended she *was* a pelican, she had the walk and the sound they made down pat. She tried for a long, long time to get that pelican to hang out with her but he was shy and reluctant and then finally she asked me to lie on the beach like a dead fish that she could pretend to be eating and maybe that would tempt the pelican to come on over. I tried to act like a dead fish but I was laughing too hard to be convincing. Min was pretending to peck at me and it tickled like crazy and even though she was whispering at me out of the side of her beak to be quiet and act dead I couldn't stop laughing. Finally she said okay, forget it, this isn't working, let's tan.

We lay together in the sun and I fell asleep and when I woke up I was feeling cold and she'd taken her towel and put it around my shoulders and then rubbed my back and arms to warm me up. She smiled at me and told me that she was really happy that I was her sister. You were a great pelican, I told her. Yeah, no, she said, but thanks. I was a terrible fish, I said. No, she said, you were an excellent fish, A-plus, just not a good dead one. She told me she was proud of me.

I didn't know if she meant because I had agreed to pretend to be a dead fish so that she could befriend a pelican, but I didn't care.

We were just a few miles out of Calexico, in a place called El Centro. I'm gonna make one more super-quick stop for gas, I said. You guys just wait in the van.

May I speak to Min Troutman, please? I said.

Min isn't here any more, said the desk nurse.

What do you mean? I said.

She discharged herself this afternoon, she said.

What do you mean? I said.

She'll continue getting treatment as an outpatient, said the woman.

Yeah, but, what do you *mean*? I said.

She went home today, said the woman.

Yeah, but there's nobody there. She told me you'd only let her out if there was somebody there to help her, I said.

She told us there *was* somebody there, said the woman. I think she said it was her sister.

I phoned the house. There was no answer. Just the machine with Thebes going, *Bonjourno! The Troutmans are outie. Leave a message but it better be good.*

Min, it's me, Hattie. Are you there? Can you pick up the phone if you're there? I told her that the kids and I were fine, just out on a short road trip, we'd be back soon, and I asked her again if she was there, but there was no response. If she was there she wasn't picking up the phone, which wasn't unusual, she never answered the phone. Are you really not there? I asked again. Just wait for me, I said. Just hold on.

Ready? I said to the kids.

For what? said Logan.

Just . . . I don't know, for this, I said.

Well, yeah, said Logan. The whole point is—

I know, I said. Thebie? Ready?

Rock 'n' roll, she said.

I looked at her in the rear-view mirror. Her hair was up Smurf-style again and she'd stuck glitter to her cheeks and eyelids.

Why is your lip bleeding? said Logan.

I don't know, I said. I think I bit it by accident. Hey, put in a CD.

Which one?

I don't care, whatever, I said.

He flipped through his CDs and put one in.

Is this your favourite band? I said.

No, he said. But I like them.

What is it, like emo or something? I said.

Kind of, he said.

Turn it up, I said. I didn't want Thebes to hear what I was saying.

Logan, I said.

Hattie, he said.

We're just gonna say hi to Cherkis, hang out awhile and then blast. We have to go home.

Yeah, said Logan. Hmmmm. He was scratching inside his cast again.

Min's out of the hospital, I said. They said she went home and I tried calling her but I only got the machine.

She hardly ever answers the phone, said Logan.

Yeah, I know, I said.

She's probably okay, said Logan. Now he was carving into the dashboard.

Yeah, I know, I said. But the thing I'm trying to say is that I'm not going to leave you guys with Cherkis, even if he does say it's all right with him.

Okay, said Logan. That's cool.

What are you writing? I asked him.

The date, he said.

Well, you might as well sign it too, I said.

Fine, he said. Beneath the date, he wrote *the f—ing Troutmans*. Thebes popped up from the back seat and watched him carve. When he was done, he snapped his knife shut and changed the CD. Thebes yanked the cap off her glitter pen, leaned forward and changed the signature so it read *the flying Troutmans.*

We pulled onto a narrow dirt road next to a bunch of tents pitched right up by the border and we all got out of the van, broken, cut, bleeding, bruised and filthy and armed with small, dull knives, toy pistols, concealed scalpels and a pit bull that somewhere along the way had lost its killer instinct.

It's not Paris, said Logan.

We walked across the sand, through scrubby bushes, and up to a group of people sitting around cooking something on a camp stove.

Cherkis looked up and stared at us.

How's it going? I asked him.

Holy shit, he said.

Hi, said Logan.

Thebes looked at Cherkis and smiled shyly and dug her toes into the sand and then cleared her throat but didn't say a word.

This is Thebes, here, I said. And Logan.

Yeah, said Cherkis, I know. I mean I figured it out. I'm just . . . I don't know what to say. Wow! You guys are so . . . big! Sorry, he said. He started crying. Then he started laughing, wiping tears from his cheeks, apologizing again, and we all laughed nervously together, while Thebes kicked up tiny clouds of dirt.

Cherkis jumped up and came closer. He was smaller than I remembered him being. Skinny like the kids and constantly in motion. He was wearing a dirty black T-shirt and jeans and big motorcycle boots. His hair was really dark but there was a streak of silver in it. He opened his mouth and closed it again and shook his head and then put his arms out.

Man, am I happy to see you guys, he said, just like the way Logan had dreamed it, kind of, except that it had been my father popping out of the ocean and not his popping out of the sand. Logan put his arms around his father and Cherkis motioned for Thebes to join them in their awkward embrace. She looked up at me and I pointed to the guys and she moved towards them and they held one another in a huddle. I watched them and I asked myself again, the way Thebie had as Logan's fake basketball coach, *Who do you have, Hattie?* And I answered, Min.

I sat down and introduced myself to the others sitting in the sand. We made small talk and I tried to explain what we were doing there. Then I left them and wandered over to a drunk guy, a comrade, laid out on a blanket and asked him if I could sit there in the shade with him for a few minutes. He said the thing to do is drink 'til you don't can't. He didn't ask me who I was or what I was doing there and I gave thanks to the universe. If I were to move in a love direction, I asked him, which way do you think it would be?

Cherkis finally let go of his kids and went running off to his tent and brought out a whole bunch of photos of Thebes and Logan when they were little.

There's you, he said to Logan, when you were Superman on Halloween. You're three years old in this picture. You were so sad when you had to go to bed. Min and I had some friends over and you were crying your eyes out and waving goodbye to everyone and saying, but everybody knows I'm Superman. Logan stared at the photo.

And there's you, Thebes, with your underwear on your head.

Cherkis showed Thebes and Logan all the pictures and told them the stories behind them.

Hey, said Cherkis, how'd you get that cast on your arm? Logan shrugged and said he didn't know. Things break? said Cherkis. Logan smiled.

Thebes asked Cherkis if he'd be interested in an over-sized novelty cheque and he said oh yeah, more than anything.

The anarchists had a Ping-Pong table set up and we played a wacky game where everyone gets a turn. You hit the ball and then throw the paddle down, take a few steps sideways, and the next person picks it up and hits the ball when it comes back. If someone had seen us from the air it would have looked like some kind of tribal dance around a green square with white lines on it.

Then Logan and Cherkis went off into the desert for a walk and talk, and Thebes flew the kite she'd made for me and let everyone have a turn. We all watched her wave and smile at us from three hundred feet in the air. After that she ran over to the van and got the fireworks she and Logan had bought and when Cherkis and Logan came back we set them off.

We watched them explode in space and float back to earth, and Cherkis explained to Thebes what he was doing there at the border. We count the go-backs, the ones who stay and linger on the line and the ones who make a break for it, he said. We count them all.

Hey, Cherkis, I said, can I talk to you alone for a minute?

C'mon, Thebie, said Logan, let's play a game of Ping-Pong. I'll use my left hand.

Cherkis and I walked over to the van and sat down on the back bumper. It was really dark there. He switched off his flashlight and we stared at the stars.

Min's not doing well, I said, not at all.

I know, said Cherkis, Logan told me.

Yeah, I don't even know exactly where she is right now, I said.

I know, said Cherkis.

I have to go home and find her, I said. I want to leave tonight. I know we just got here . . .

Yeah, it's okay, said Cherkis. I asked Logan if he wanted to stay with me for the summer and he said yeah, he'd love to.

He did? I said. But . . .

Yeah, he said he'd love to but that he couldn't because he had to get back to take care of Thebes and Min. He said you were probably heading back to Paris.

Hey, I said, can you hang on for just a minute?

Cherkis shrugged and said he had all the time in the world.

I ran over to the Ping-Pong table and asked Logan if I could talk to him alone for a second. I hustled him off into the shadows and asked him if it was true, if he really wanted to hang out there with Cherkis for the summer. He said yeah, but he wasn't going to, obviously.

But, wait, I said, why don't you? You should! If you want to, you should.

Well, no . . . my mom . . . and there's Thebes . . . so . . .

Okay, I said. You should stay. However Min deals with it isn't your problem. It'll be my problem, okay? You should hang out with your dad for a while if that's what you want to do. Thebes and I will go back and I'll take care of her and Min and I'll explain to your mom that you love her, that you haven't left her, and that you're coming back for school in the fall. That's only a couple of months away.

Yeah, but . . . , said Logan.

Seriously, Logan, I said. It would be fun. You should be having fun. I'm gonna stay with Min and Thebes for as long as they need me, probably longer. I'm not going back to Paris. You just stay here and get to know Cherkis. Do you want to?

Yeah, said Logan. But—

Okay, I said. You're fifteen. Take care of yourself. You can worry about the rest of us sometimes, a bit, if you have to, but it's not your job to take care of Min or Thebes. It's my job. I want the job. I promise I'll take care of them, but promise me you'll take care of yourself?

Well, said Logan, I guess . . . He smiled. A beautiful, heart-stopping smile, all badly disguised tenderness and tentative joy.

Yeah? I said. I smiled back. I punched him on the shoulder. I didn't know what else to do.

Okay, he said, sounds good. He punched me back and

then, strangely, he picked me right up off the ground and twirled me around for a second or two.

Hey, are you freaks dancing? It was Thebes.

Yeah, I said.

No, said Logan. He put me down.

Let's finish our Ping-Pong game, T., he said.

I ran back to Cherkis to tell him that Logan would spend the summer with him after all.

Really? he said. Really? Well, that's . . . what about Thebes?

No, she wants to go back, I said. But she's having a blast right now. I think—

Do you think Min will be okay with her? he asked.

I don't know, I said. But I'll be there too. I'm not going back to Paris. I asked him if he knew where the nearest airport was.

I guess San Diego, said Cherkis. It's about a hundred miles from here.

Do you want the van? I said. You and Logan can use it for the summer.

Well, but, does he have a licence? asked Cherkis.

No, not technically, I said, but he knows what he's doing, mostly. I asked Cherkis if he could drive me and Thebes to San Diego that night. If we were lucky we could be with Min the next day, if she was at home. If she wasn't at home, I'd find her. I had found Cherkis, after all, I could find Min. I remembered something weird that Logan had written on the back of a parking ticket I found in the glove compartment. *Part of me is missing, but I will find the enemy and destroy him!* I hadn't known what he meant, but maybe now I could start to piece it together. We were all playing an elaborate game of Hide-and-Seek.

And would you mind keeping Rajbeer too? I asked him.

A son, a van and a dog, he said. Anything else?

He shone the flashlight into my face for a second and I closed my eyes and smiled and told him no, that was it for now. Although, I couldn't guarantee that his two daughters wouldn't want to stay with him someday too.

No guarantee, he agreed. He asked me how Antonia and Lilah were doing and I told him they were fine and missed him.

I miss them too, said Cherkis. I miss everybody.

Then I told Cherkis a story about a day I'd spent years ago with Min and the kids, shortly after she'd run him out of town. She was away visiting some friends in Washington and I was looking after Logan and Thebes. Logan was about four and Thebes was just a baby, still nursing. Min had spent hours pumping breast milk and putting it all into small glass bottles that she marked *Property of Theodora Troutman.* She hadn't really wanted to leave the kids but one of her friends was getting married and wanted her to be there and I was happy to stay with them. It was just for a few days.

So the day she came back it was her birthday, and it was a beautiful, sunny day and Thebes and Logan and I went to the airport to pick her up. Thebes was too young to understand much but Logan was really excited about seeing her again and was running around and jumping up and down in the waiting area, wearing little sneakers that flashed when he ran. I had put a bright pink dress and sunhat on Thebes and I was helping her walk around and around while we waited, holding her hands because she couldn't quite do it on her own yet.

There was this glass wall separating us from the arriving passengers but we could see them coming. So, then, there was Min. We were all waving and smiling at each other. She looked really happy. And beautiful too. She was wearing this goofy orange beret and a long gauzy skirt. But then she had to stop at an official-looking desk before she could come through the door to the area where we were waiting, and so she had to turn her back to us for a minute while she was talking to the guy behind the desk. Logan asked me why she wasn't coming out and I said I didn't know exactly, but then someone standing beside us said that the desk was where arriving passengers had to pay the airport tax. I had never heard of it.

So, anyway, Min was talking to the guy for quite a long time, every so often turning around and smiling and waving or making these cartoony expressions of frustration, rolling her eyes a lot, and we'd all smile and wave back, but we didn't know why she wasn't coming out. And then, suddenly, Min was throwing her beret to the floor and she was dancing. She had turned to face us as she danced, and the kids both laughed and giggled while she did this comic combination of tap and ballet and the guy standing next to me asked me what she was doing and I said well, she's dancing, looks like, and he said yeah, okay, cool. And then we saw Min look at a few passengers walking past her and she pointed at her hat and kept on dancing, and it was really beautiful in this odd way, like a silent film, because we couldn't hear anything, and her gauzy skirt and all her hair was swirling around, and the kids were loving it.

And then some of those passengers started to smile at her and reach into their pockets and pull out change and bills and throw them into her hat. Some of them clapped, and Logan did too, and he told the guy next to us that that was his mom, the one dancing, and the guy said she was great, Logan was lucky.

Finally, she must have figured she had enough money, because she stopped dancing and dumped all the change onto the desk and it looked like the guy was counting it and then he nodded and I guess told her she could finally go, and she turned around and curtseyed and smiled and pretended to brush some imaginary dust off her hands and came through the glass wall to meet us.

Now Cherkis was crying and I took his hand and we stood around and watched the kids play under this big trouble light they'd strung up from poles. Some smaller fireworks were still going off and Rajbeer was running around, barking like crazy. Cherkis and I watched the white Ping-Pong ball bounce back and forth across the net for a while, it was kind of mesmerizing, and then Thebes spiked it hard and it hit Logan right between the eyes, and he laughed and the ball went spinning off into the darkness like a tiny plastic universe out of control.

acknowledgments

Thank you to my editor Michael Schellenberg for his magic and to my agent, Carolyn Swayze, for her tenacity. And to both for their patience. And to my beautiful and intrepid family and friends for their enduring love and, on that note, especially to NCR for moving mountains.

MIRIAM TOEWS is the author of three previous novels: *Summer of My Amazing Luck*; *A Boy of Good Breeding* and *A Complicated Kindness* (winner of the 2004 Governor's General Award for fiction) and one work of non-fiction: *Swing Low: A Life*. She lives in Winnipeg.